MY PERFECT SALVATION

Perfect Series, Book Two

By: Kenadee Bryant

MY PERFECT SALVATION

Limitless Publishing, LLC
Kailua, HI 96734
www.limitlesspublishing.com

Formatting: Limitless Publishing

ISBN-13: 978-1-64034-187-6
ISBN-10: 1-64034-187-0

Dedication

To everyone on Wattpad who read and supported this book.

Chapter 1

Layla

Before I knew it, it was Thursday—the day before the benefit gala. The last week and a half flew by with my running all over the place trying to get everything ready for that night. I had made hundreds upon hundreds of calls to different venues, caterers, party guests, and the place where the invitations were being made. And on top of that, I still had to do everything for Ashton at work, with meetings, filing, reports, and running stupid errands for him. I hadn't slept very much in the last week. I didn't leave the office until eight on most nights, sometimes even staying until nine or ten. I was exhausted but I had to make this gala amazing, or Ashton would win and I would look stupid and incompetent.

A few days into the project, I wondered why I was the only one doing all the work and he didn't have others doing stuff too. I was tempted to ask Judy why, but I thought she would talk to Ashton about it and that was the last thing I wanted. I didn't want him thinking I couldn't handle it. Most days I almost missed lunch, but Neena had gotten in the habit of calling and texting me over and over again until I came down to the cafeteria with her. If it weren't for her, I probably wouldn't eat all day. I had found out that Neena was *very* sarcastic and seemed to say whatever was on her mind most of the time. On Monday, when Neena and I went to lunch, Liam surprisingly came and ate with us. Neena had seen him a few times but never talked to him, so when he took a seat at our table, she almost choked on her drink. She wouldn't admit it, but she was smitten with the data processor.

Liam and Neena were my only friends at work, and I was okay with that. They were both great to talk to and kept my mind off of a certain someone. When Neena came over during the weekend, her and Kacey immediately clicked. They sat down on the couch and talked about fashion for a good hour before I interrupted them, bored out of my mind. Since that night, Neena seemed to come into our friendship and we were now the three amigos. Kacey, of course, was still Kacey. Every night before bed, she laid something out for me to wear, and they probably weren't the best outfits to wear to work but since I had nothing else, I wore them. She also made me promise once this gala was over and I got paid, we were going shopping. She had it in her mind that if I showed a lot of skin, Ashton would come running back apologizing, and she had it totally wrong. All week he never once looked at me; he only did when he bossed me around.

2

Even during meetings with board members, clients, or other supervisors, he kept his distance and his gaze far away from me. Whenever he did look at me, it was with disgust and almost loathing. I guess I was really that terrible looking and disgusting that he regretted ever touching me. I swallowed down the pain every day and ignored the ache in my chest that seemed to grow every time he asked me to book him a reservation at some fancy restaurant, or when I went to his apartment and found a pair of woman's panties on his bedside table. I took all of that in stride, but the other day when he came into work and had lipstick smeared on his neck and around his mouth, I lost it. I locked myself in my office for a good hour before forcing all of my feelings down and got back to work. It was safe to say my heart had a pretty good crack in it by now. I was happy now that I hadn't slept with him, or the pain would be worse.

Both Neena and Kacey didn't like that Ashton was using me and making me do this whole gala by myself. They both threatened to kick Ashton's ass. After telling them I was fine and practically yelling at them both to stop, they did but rather reluctantly. They still said stuff about Ashton every day, but luckily didn't do anything. I agreed with them, but I needed this job, and I felt like I needed to prove myself to everyone.

Back in high school, I was the quiet, shy nerd with the popular best friend. I didn't socialize much, thanks to my parents mostly, and kids tended to pick on me more than others. I never told Kacey that people did, and that most were her friends on

3

the cheerleading squad. While Kacey was cheer co-captain, student body officer, and was outgoing and friendly, I was the total opposite. I never did any sports, I stayed home more often than not, and I was quiet around people. Maybe it was because I didn't want people to find out what my parents did to me, or maybe it was because my parents threatened me that, if anyone found out about how they abused me, they would do something way worse than usual. I feared that if I got out of my shell the spotlight would turn to me and shine down on my family and how terrible my home life was. So, I stayed the social hermit and let Kacey have all the spotlight.

Once I moved out and went to college, I kind of became a different person. Being away from my abusive family was the best thing that could have happened to me. I came out of my shell and loosened up a bit more. I was more outgoing and actually went to parties with Kacey. My first year of college I got my very first boyfriend, Jason Wells, and I couldn't be happier. He was on the school's football team, very cute, and about a year older than me. He had blonde hair that was a little on the long side, and had a pair of really pretty green eyes, and a very fine body. I was one of those girls who had the hottest boyfriend and was a nerd. We got along great, and he helped me become more confident and social. Well, I kind of had to be when I was dating the school's star running back.

Jason managed to push down my walls and wedged himself inside. And for once, I was completely and utterly happy. He didn't seem to care about my past and the huge scar I had on my

4

stomach. He liked me for me. Being a happy and naive nineteen-year-old, I lost my virginity to him. We dated for almost two years; I was in the middle of my junior year and he was a senior. Everything in my life was going great. My grades were high, I hadn't heard from my parents, Kacey was happy with her own boyfriend, and I was in love. I remember the day when my whole split in two, like it just happened yesterday.

It was the day of our anniversary; we had been together for two years. I had gotten all ready, dressed up in a tight short dress cause that's what he liked. My hair was curled perfectly, and my makeup was on point. I had never gotten this dressed up before, but I wanted this night to be perfect. For our special day, I went and spent my last three paychecks and bought him a specially signed football by his favorite quarterback. I had searched for weeks to find one and when I did, it was a lot of money. At the time, I was working on campus and only made so much but I wanted to get Jason something nice, so I bought it. I wrapped it all nice and made a card telling him how much I loved him and how he had changed my life. He told me he would pick me up at six and take me somewhere that was a surprise. Six came and went. I sat on my couch waiting and looking at the door every five seconds.

Soon it was eight and he still hadn't shown up. Wondering what was taking so long, I sent him a text and waited. When eight thirty hit and there was still no reply, I decided to check his room. Maybe something had happened and he left his phone at home. Thankfully his dorm room wasn't too far from mine, so I walked there in five minutes. With his present under one arm, I knocked on his door. When no answer came, I tried again. This time I heard shuffling through the door and a few grunts and moans. Confused, I put my hand on the door handle and found it unlocked. The voice in the back of my head was yelling and telling me not to go in there, but I ignored it. I pushed through the door and immediately froze.

There on the bed was my boyfriend and some blonde. I recognized her from the cheer team but couldn't think of her name. They were both stark naked and didn't even seem to notice me there. They kept going at it as I stood there frozen and watched. My eyes filled with tears as I realized he was here fucking some other girl while I sat at home waiting for him to come pick me up, and on our anniversary. I must have gasped or something, because both of their heads snapped to my direction. Jason's green eyes widened as he took me in staring at them.

"Layla—" he started to say but I just shook my head at him.

"So, this is what you were doing instead of picking me up for our anniversary?" I said, surprised my voice came out strong instead of small like how I was feeling. He pushed the blonde to the side and went to stand up, a sheet wrapped around his bare waist.

"Babe."

"Don't 'babe' me. I am not your babe

6

anymore," I said, my voice neutral despite the anger and hurt. I should have known this was too good to be true. "Happy anniversary." With that, I set his gift on the table by the door and walked out slamming the door behind me. I walked down the hall blindly as tears streamed down my face. I somehow made my way home and collapsed on my bed, sobbing.

It was pretty ironic how I was in the same position only a week ago. After the day I found him, I went back to being a shell. Jason only bugged me for a few days before he stopped and he never talked to me again. After Jason, I only went on a few dates but never had a serious relationship. I became who I once was, and I didn't want to become like that again. It took me months to get back to semi-normal and even then, I wasn't the same. That was why, this time with Ashton, I was determined I wasn't going to do that again and that I was going to prove to everyone and myself I was stronger now than I was before. This gala was going to show that I could do things myself and that I wasn't easily broken. Friday's gala was going to be the best one this company had ever had, and it would be all thanks to me.

That was why I was here sitting in Ashton's office writing down his speech for him. I wanted to ignore him completely, but being his PA and in charge of everything, I had to make sure his speech was written and done. Ashton had to give the opening speech Friday, and it had to be good. We have been going at it for an hour and thankfully we were about done. Only a few more sentences to wrap it all up. It was times like these I was glad my handwriting was pretty good. It would suck for Ashton if my handwriting sucked and he had to read it.

Ashton sat there looking out his window, not saying anything as I caught up writing what he told me to. The tension in the air was almost palpable and I wanted out of this office quickly. It was past five-thirty, and my stomach was growling constantly. Who knew this job would make me this hungry? You would think I had a physical job, but my old job was worse than this and I wasn't nearly as hungry. I was starting to think they put pot in the food so you would keep coming to get more.

Being the writer that I am, or, well, want to be, I had put extra words into Ashton's speech along with some extra sentences to sound better. Noticing that Ashton wasn't paying attention to me, I finished his speech off for him. Quickly re-reading through it, I deemed it good and set it down on his desk. I stood up, ready to go home. I needed as much sleep as I could get, since tomorrow was the gala. I had a thousand things to do tomorrow at work, then I had to get ready and head to the place to gala was being held to make sure everything was set up at exactly seven, before the guests arrived. I didn't want to attend, but I had to be there to make sure security was in place, that the food was done on time and that there was enough, that the tables were finished and set, and that people who were making speeches and auctioning off stuff was done correctly. I wasn't even planning on dressing up; I was just going to wear what I would wear to work. It wasn't like I was important enough to be there anyways.

"Is that all, Mr. Miller?" I asked, straightening out my things.

"I need you to cancel all of my appointments tomorrow and reschedule them. I won't be in all day," he said, not looking at me. *Great, just great. More work for me.*

"Sure thing. Anything else?" I saw him shake his head, so I stood up and straightened my skirt. "Make sure you are there a little bit before seven," I said.

"Make sure you don't wear anything revealing; not that it's going to be hard, seeing the way you are. I don't want people talking about how much of a slut my assistant is. And if this gala is terrible, it is on your head. Not mine," Ashton said out of the blue. I froze and stared at him. Did he just say I was a slut and that I would be fired if this gala was bad? My chest ached, as his words hurt me. I bit back my retort.

"Yes, sir," I bit out and left his office. There were so many things I wanted to say to Ashton. Most were swear words and the others were questions as to why he was treating me like shit now. Forcing myself to leave the building instead of turning around and giving Ashton a piece of my mind was hard to do. As I got in a taxi and headed home, I couldn't help but think.

Just you wait, Ashton. Just you wait.

Chapter 2

Layla

I got up the next morning later than I wanted, and I hustled to get ready. I had so much to do today that I couldn't be late to the office. Slipping on a pencil skirt and a black blouse, I brushed my hair and left it to be somewhat wavy. I put only a little bit of makeup on to hide the dark circles under my eyes and to make my cheeks look like they had some life in them. Grabbing the heels I had claimed as my own by now, I grabbed my stuff and was out the door. I was not looking forward to today. I just wanted it to go by fast so I could have the weekend to relax.

As I headed to the office, I was slightly excited because I would finally be getting paid. It was pretty stupid of me not to ask Ashton what the pay was like and when I would get my check, but like everything else, I found out on my own. Since I had missed the pay deadline the week I started, I had to wait an extra two weeks to get paid. Thankfully I had money saved from my old job to last me until this paycheck. After everything that I had been doing these past two weeks, it would be nice to see that hard work paying off.

You could tell it was a Friday because people were dressed somewhat casual, and there seemed to be excitement in the air. I walked into the building at six exactly, and talked to Neena briefly before I went upstairs to get to work. The list of things I had to do today went on for miles, and I knew if I didn't get my work stuff done then I would be here over the weekend and I didn't want that. I had to come in on Sunday last weekend to finish up some stuff, and I didn't want to have to do that again. I needed a full weekend of relaxation to make up for a hectic two weeks.

The moment I stepped into my office I got to work. If anyone would have seen me, they would have thought I had been working here for years instead of two and a half weeks. I flew across my office and down the halls quicker than anyone usually could in four-inch heels. I was like a demon-possessed woman as I zoomed through the work I needed to get done. I had never felt so overwhelmed or rushed in my life, not even in college.

After rescheduling all of Ashton's appointments, re-filing new paper work, and sending them to a supervisor on floor fifteen, I grabbed my stuff to go pick up Ashton's suit for tonight. It was almost noon, so I knew I had to hurry to the suit place just in case they closed for lunch. I passed Judy's desk before she yelled my name.

"Layla!" she called after me. I turned and walked back to her desk.

"Yeah?" I asked.

"Your check is in." She handed me an envelope with my name. "Since you haven't filled out on your W-2, if you wanted direct deposit or a check, I just told them to put it directly into your account. If you want, you can change it later too. It's not a big deal," she said, smiling at me.

"Thanks!" I said, smiling down at the envelope. "Sorry to just run off on you, but I have to get going. You're coming to the Gala tonight, right?" I asked as I stepped back. I couldn't remember who I had sent invitations to. All Ashton did was email me a long list of names that consisted of two hundred people, maybe more. I had just printed it and sent it to the invitation place to be made. I didn't even look at the names. Thankfully, though, most of the staff here would be attending, so that gave me Neena and Liam to talk to even though I would be working.

"Of course. I have to make sure Ashton doesn't do something stupid," she said with a smile. I giggled and waved at her.

"See you tonight then if I'm not back in time," I called and hurried to the elevator.

As I walked outside, I saw Clark's car idling near the curb. I raised an eyebrow and walked over to him.

"Clark, I thought you were with Ashton today?" I asked.

"No, ma'am. He instructed me to give you a ride anywhere you needed to go today," Clark said, opening the door. I smashed down the feeling of happiness bubbling in my chest. Ashton didn't do it out of anything but my necessity. At least he wasn't going to make me pay for a taxi to drive me all over hell. I sent Clark a thankful smile and got in the car.

"Where to, Ms. Kingston?" he asked, getting into the driver's seat.

"The dry cleaner's again. I have to pick up a suit for Ashton tonight. And call me Layla," I said to Clark.

"As you wish, Layla," Clark said and started driving toward our destination. As we drove, silence laced through the car and I couldn't help but fidget in my seat.

"So…how long have you been working for Ashton?" I asked, breaking the silence. I didn't do well when it was completely silent. When I was by myself, I was fine, but with others, I always felt the need to blab about random stuff. I was very guilty of word vomit.

"About five years."

"That's when he took over the company, right?" I asked.

"Yes." His answer was short. *Nice conversation,* I thought sarcastically. Clark wasn't much of a talker apparently. I clamped my lips shut on the words that were dying to break free. Fortunately, the car came to a stop a few minutes later. I looked out the window and turned to Clark.

"Would you mind coming in with me? I have to pick out a suit and I could use your opinion," I asked. I would admit I should have done this a couple of days ago, but with everything going on, I forgot about it until last night. I was just hoping they had some good suits left, seeing this was the place to go in New York. Clark just nodded and got out. Before he could open my door for me, I opened it and stepped out.

I entered the place with Clark behind me and started toward the back. I didn't know Ashton's size, but I figured they would since Ashton took his suits here to be cleaned. As I came to a stop in front of the desk, I saw the same man from last time.

"Excuse me?" I asked. He looked up at me and then his gaze shifted to Clark, who stood behind me. Honestly, Clark was pretty intimidating. His brown hair was buzzed short, and he had very wide shoulders, making me wonder how he fit in the car. He looked like an ex-wrestler or bodyguard. I didn't know why I just now noticed how he looked, but I did and I realized he was big.

"Yes, miss?" the man asked, taking his gaze off of Clark. He seemed to kind of recognize me.

"I am here looking for a suit for Mr. Miller." After I said his name, the man's eyes lit up. "I was wondering if you could show me some of your selections in his size?"

"Oh, yes! Right this way," the man said energetically. *Wow, they must really value Ashton's business.* "My name is Martin," he said as he led us to a section even further in the back. "These are our best selections."

I stood in front of a big rack full of different colors, and styles of suits. *This is going to be hard. I have never picked out a suit before.* I shot Martin a smile and started going through the selections. I didn't know if he wanted a plain black one or maybe a gray one. *Damnit, I really should have done this sooner.* I looked over at Clark for some help.

"What color do you think?" I asked, biting my bottom lip and staring at the rack. All Clark did was shrug. I shot him a glare and turned back to the suits. "Some kind of help you are," I muttered under my breath. Moving around, my eyes were suddenly drawn to one over on another shelf.

It was a deep blue color with lighter blue lines within it. The blue wasn't too dark to be black, and the lighter blue was a tasteful contrast. For some reason, it screamed Ashton to me. In the back of my mind, I could see him in it and his deep blue eyes shining even more. I ran my hand over it, and it felt so smooth and soft at the same time. Turning, I nodded to Martin.

"This one," was all I said. I glanced over at Clark and saw him sending me a small nod of approval.

"Perfect! And that is our last one in that size. Do you need a tie as well?" Martin went and grabbed it off the rack and headed to put it in case.

"Oh no, I think we are good." I bet Ashton had enough ties to find one to match.

"How much will it be?" I asked once he was finished.

"No worries, we will just bill it to Mr. Miller's usual card," he said, waving. Yes, one less thing I had to deal with. "Here you are. Thank you for shopping with us." Thanking him, I followed Clark in the car and directed him to Ashton's apartment. On the way to Ashton's house, I called the venue, The Smith's Center, to make sure everything was being delivered and decorations were being put up. Since it was after noon and I had practically everything taken care of at the office, I would have Clark drop me off at the venue. That way, I could help if needed.

Clark pulled up to Ashton's apartment, and I quickly got out and headed to the elevator. My stomach grumbled but I didn't have time to stop and eat. I rubbed my stomach, trying to calm it down. When I was hungry, my stomach loved to make whale noises that were really embarrassing. Missing one meal wasn't anything compared to when I was in high school. I would sometimes go a week or more with no food.

Typing in the code once I got to his door, I walked inside and headed to his room. Every time I come here I was still amazed by the size. It was easily two of my apartments put together, maybe even more. These past two weeks Ashton had made me run stupid personal errands for him. Thankfully, though, he hasn't sent me out to buy condoms or anything like that. If he would have done that, I think I might have quit or said something very inappropriate.

I set his suit on his bed to make sure he would wear it tonight and glanced around. I didn't want to stay in here longer than I had to. I could practically see all the times he brought girls in here and had his way with them on the very bed I slept on when I first met him. Sighing, I left his room and headed back to the car. I had a benefit gala to go help with.

***

Three hours later, I was ready to pull my hair out. Everything seemed to be going wrong. The barista called in sick, so I had to hurry and call someone else to show up. The decorations and place settings were set up all wrong, so I personally had to redo all one hundred of them. Name cards were set at the wrong tables, and people who I knew wouldn't sit next to so and so had to be moved. Multiple pieces being auctioned off were late. And security was less than I wanted because one guy had a family emergency and a few others were needed somewhere else more important. I was currently on the phone with the catering wondering where they were.

"I need you here now, not in two hours! The benefit starts at exactly seven." I interrupted the lady through the phone. I knew I was being rude but it seemed to be the only way to get things done around here. *God, New Yorkers are hard to deal with,* I thought. After almost yelling bloody murder at the lady, she said she would be there in twenty minutes with all the food. I slumped against the wall and rubbed my forehead. My head was pounding, and I knew by the end of the night I would have a migraine.

"Everything's going perfect I see," said a deep voice in front of me. I opened my eyes and shot Clark a glare. I was actually surprised at his sarcastic comment. A reaction other than a nod or worded one-word answer.

"Oh yeah, perfectly. Everything is just fine and dandy!" I said sarcastically in reply.

"Everything looks great though. It will be a

splendid party." Clark said.

"Did you just say 'splendid'?" I asked, raising an eyebrow at him. He shrugged, but I saw a small smile gracing his lips. "But thank you."

"May I ask, though. Where is everyone else?" I glanced at him, confused.

"Everyone else?"

"Yes, other people to help. It seems you are the only one doing everything."

"That's because I am the only one," I said tiredly. What I really wanted to do was go home, lie in a bubble bath, and put on my PJs watching reruns of Friends.

"Wait? You have had to do everything for this party? No one else?" I nodded in response to all his questions, confused by his tone. He seemed shocked and confused finding that out. Before I could ask him why he was so confused, my phone rang loudly echoing through the hall.

"Hello?" I asked not glancing at the caller ID.

"Layla, where are you? You need to get home so we can get ready!" Kacey said through my phone.

"Kacey, I'm still working. I wasn't even planning on wearing anything besides what I have on anyways," I replied, closing my eyes and pinching the bridge of my nose.

"Oh, hell no! You are dressing up whether you agree or not. I will knock you out if I have to," Kacey threatened.

I sighed. "I'm busy here, Kay. Clark and I still have a lot to do," I said Clark's name to hopefully get her to know I'm serious but it had the opposite effect.

"Give Clark the phone."

My eyebrows rose, but I handed Clark the phone. He sent me a questioning look, but I just shrugged. Kacey knew Clark was Ashton's driver since I told her, but I had no idea why she needed to speak to him. I watched his face closely and inched closer, hoping to catch whatever she was telling him but Clark's face was emotionless and by the time I got close enough, he hung up the phone.

"Layla, it's best we get going. You need to get ready," Clark said.

"Wait, what did Kacey tell you?" I asked as I followed behind him. I knew I had to follow because if I didn't, she wouldn't hesitate to come all the way here to drag me back to the apartment to get ready.

"Let's just say I value certain parts of my body," he said and opened the car door for me. I choked on my laughter as I slid inside. Only Kacey would threaten someone like Clark. The drive to my apartment was quick and before I knew it, I was being hauled inside by Kacey.

I stumbled against her and tried to find my footing, but she dragged me all the way to my room.

"Shower and then come to my room," she said, pushing through my bedroom door. "And thoroughly!" With that, she left me to shower and headed back to do whatever she was doing while I showered.

As I quickly showered, I did what she asked. I shaved my legs again although I already did two days ago, shaved my under arms, and made sure to wash my hair really good. After about fifteen minutes, I was out. Stepping out the warm shower, I wrapped a towel around my body and brushed my wet hair. I pulled on a pair of panties before heading to Kacey's room. I didn't know what she had planned and I was sort of fearful. As soon as I stepped into her room, the doorbell rang.

"I got it," she said and brushed past me. Like I was going to open the door only wearing a towel. I sat on the edge of her bed and she came in a minute later followed by Neena.

"Hey, Layla," Neena said and came to sit by me.

"Hey, what are you doing here?" I asked.

"You don't want me here? I get it; you don't love me," she said, grabbing her chest and falling back on the bed. "You wound me." I chuckled at her and hit her with a small pillow I found behind me.

"She's here to get ready with us," Kacey said, going through her over stuffed closet.

"Wait, 'us?'"

"Seriously, where have you been? I am going to be Neena's 'guest.' Like hell I'm going to let you guys go to this without me. Now, Layla, come here. I need to start on your hair and make-up. Neena, you're next."

For the next hour or two, all three of us got ready for gala tonight. With strict instructions to stay still, I sat in front of her mirror for about thirty minutes—with my eyes closed I might add—while Kacey poked and prodded me. While I was getting worked on, Neena was moving about the room as well. She took a shower in my room because she just came from work. Kacey made me not look at myself just yet while she did Neena's and her own make-up. I sat on the edge of her bed and talked and laughed with them. Who knew getting ready for a gala could be so much fun?

Once Neena was done, she unzipped the bag that held her dress. She pulled out a beautiful yellow dress that was totally her. It was one-shouldered and had three stripes of silver sparkles. The top part was fitted but toward the bottom, it flared out and would swished against her legs. The moment she put it on I looked her up and down.

"Not trying to sound gay here, but you look absolutely stunning in that dress, Neena!" The yellow made her skin look tan, and her blue eyes popped. Kacey had kept her make-up minimal, making her look natural, and her eyes were done in a pretty smoky look that totally matched her. Neena's pixie-cut hair was straightened and slightly curved in at the tips toward her face. "I know, right?" she said and grinned at us.

"Let me get my dress on now. Layla, you're last," Kacey said, pulling out a dark purple strapless lace dress. The moment I saw it I knew it was for Kacey. She slid it on and had Neena zip her up. It was mermaid styled, where the top half was fitted and it flared out a little above the thighs. A black bow was around the waist, and lace decorated the entire thing. Kacey's make-up was a little more than Neena's but not by much, just more of a blush to her pale cheeks. Her eyeshadow was a mix of black and purple and when she blinked, her lid was sprinkled with purple sparkles.

"Wow, you look...amazing, Kay!" I knew

whatever I wore, these two girls would out shine me by a mile.

"Thank you! Now, your turn. The moment I saw this dress, I thought of you." Kacey reached into her closet and brought out a gorgeous bright red dress. My jaw dropped as I stood and touched it. It felt like fine silk and I almost didn't want to wear it in case I ruined it. With the help of Kacey, I slid it on and looked in the mirror. Standing in front of me was a totally different person. The bright red dress was a great contrast with my tan skin. The dress was mermaid styled just like Kacey's, and the top was strapless and came in helping push my boobs up higher. The bottom was ruffled and trailed behind me. Kacey had my hair curled and pinned to the side so it was over my left shoulder. My make-up was natural, and my eyeshadow was dark with a hint of red at the corners and when I blinked.

I couldn't believe that was me in the mirror. Gone was that awkward, too skinny, shy girl; in her place stood a confident, radiant, and curvy girl. My eyes welled with tears but I quickly fanned them away before I could ruin my makeup. I'm blaming being emotional on lack of sleep.

"Now, Layla, you look stunning!" Neena and Kacey both said. I turned and crushed them both into a hug not caring about our dresses.

"Thank you, guys, so much."

"You are welcome! Now hush, we have to get going!" Kacey said pulling, away and grabbing her shoes. I glanced at the clock and my eyes widened. Wow, it was thirty minutes to seven; it took us 3 hours to get ready! Grabbing my Louis Vuitton heels, I slid them on. Kacey handed me a small silvery clutch to put my things in, so I headed to my room and grabbed my phone, money, and extra lipstick. As I headed toward the door, I had to lift the bottom of my dress, and followed the girls out the door.

As we headed to the gala, I forgot about Ashton and laughed with my friends in the backseat.

Chapter 3

Layla

Neena, Kacey, and I headed to The Smith Center with excitement. Even though I would be working, I was excited to go to something like this for the first time. Neena wasn't as excited as me and Kacey, but then again, she had gone to at least two of these events. I didn't know how we managed to fit all of us and our dresses into a cab. We got to The Smith Center with fifteen minutes to spare. After paying for the cab, we walked in and I heard Kacey and Neena's intake of breath. From the corner of my eye, I saw them staring at the place and decorations with awe. My heart swelled with joy knowing I'd done so well. I had chosen a dark blue and white color scheme, which the tables matched. The walls were decorated elegantly with blue drapes, all the tables had flowers and name cards on them, and up by the makeshift stage and dance floor, a table held expensive pieces to be auctioned off. People had donated a lot of good stuff, and I was hoping they would go for a lot. This benefit gala was for the New York orphanage. There were several spots around the room where guests could write down their donations and put them in the boxes so we could send them to the orphanage.

I glanced around too and saw everything seemed to be the way it should. Guests started to slowly arrive, and I had to leave Kacey and Neena for a while to go make sure security was gone and food was being prepared. I found a hidden place to put down my clutch so I wouldn't have to carry it all night. Grabbing my phone out of it, I walked to the kitchen, my heels clicking on the floor. I spent the next fifteen minutes making sure everything was set before heading back out to the ballroom.

More and more guests were arriving and were standing around talking to others. I spotted Neena and Kacey in the middle of the room, and Liam was there as well. I weaved through the crowd and made my way to them. I came to a stop beside Kacey and shot Liam a smile. He looked dashing in his black suit, his blonde hair tousled.

"You made it," I said to him.

"Of course. Pass up free alcohol and pretty ladies? No thanks," he answered, smirking. I just rolled my eyes at him. "You look very pretty as well, Layla."

"Thank you." I shot him a smile.

"You have three sexy ladies surrounding you. You should feel ecstatic. When will this ever happen again?" Neena said to him.

"Hey! I will have you know I can get any girl I want whenever I want," Liam said, puffing out his chest. I rolled my eyes at him.

"Your grandma doesn't count," Neena shot back.

"No, I mean your sister."

"I don't have a sister, dumb-ass." These two bickered like an old married couple, I swear.

From the corner of my eye, I saw the crowd of people around us turn toward the door and stop talking. Wondering what was going on, I turned as well. Just like the Red Sea, everyone parted and in walked a very elegant older couple arm in arm. Something about them seemed familiar, but I couldn't put my finger on it. As the couple came through the door, another couple walked in. This time there was a buzz around us, mostly from women though. My breath hitched and my heart crumbled just a little bit as I saw Ashton walking in with a beautiful blonde on his arm.

Ashton was wearing the suit I had set out for him, and I had to say I did well. The blue suit looked absolutely great on him. I couldn't tell what his eyes looked like, but I bet they were shining bright tonight. He had paired the suit with a brownish tie that had small white dots on it. It was weird but fit with the blue. My eyes turned to the blonde on his arm. To say she was beautiful was an understatement; she was beyond stunning. Her blonde hair was done in waves down her back. From here I couldn't see her eyes either, but I bet they were a pretty light blue as well. She wore a gorgeous deep blue dress that was strapless and fitted, and there was a big slit on the side that showed off one of her long tan legs. Everything about her screamed model, and I knew this was the type of girl Ashton liked. Tall, blonde, beautiful, model, and probably wealthy too.

They walked toward the older couple, smiling and greeting people on the way. When Ashton stood next to the man, I instantly knew that was Mr. Miller, the founder of Miller Industries and Ashton's father. *Shit, I really should have looked at the invitations more seriously.*

"Wow, she's very hot!" Liam exclaimed next to me, his eyes glued to Ashton's date. He made an "oomph" sound and a "hey." I knew Neena had elbowed him to shut him up. Since Neena had been over to our apartment quite a bit, I finally told her that I "dated" Ashton before I became his PA. She was shocked, but after hearing everything she wasn't his biggest fan anymore. She hadn't really liked him before anyways.

"Are those his parents?" Kacey asked. I just nodded, my mouth dry because I knew I needed to head over there. From here I was severely intimidated. Ashton's mother was wearing a pretty black and silver dress that made her look stunning, and I felt almost under dressed from here.

You got this, Layla. Be polite, ignore Ashton and his blonde bimbo, and show off that you know what you're doing. Don't be a baby, Layla.

After my little pep talk, I shot all three of them an encouraging smile and headed toward Ashton and his parents. I had read about his father and found out more about his mother. She was a well-known, successful lawyer. Even his sister was a successful lawyer and she was barely my age. The smart gene surely hit this family like a freight train, same with the genetics I saw on display as I got closer. It seemed everyone in his family was very attractive, I hadn't seen his sister and didn't know if she was coming, but I knew she would be drop dead gorgeous as well. With clammy hands and the need to throw up, I came to a stop in front of the four. Plastering on a smile, I greeted them.

"Hi, Mr. and Mrs. Miller. I am Layla Kingston, Ashton's assistant," I said, reaching to shake their hands. I ignored the feeling of Ashton's eyes roaming down my body.

"Hello, my dear. You look absolutely breathtaking," Ashton's father said, shaking my hand and pulling it up to place a kiss on my knuckles. I could feel the blush spreading across my cheeks. "You can just call me John. And this is my lovely wife, Clare," he said, smiling over at Ashton's mother. He looked at her with so much love that I felt kind of jealous. Even after being together for years, they are still in love. I couldn't remember if my parents ever looked at each other like that, but then again, I never was around my parents much once they started to abuse me.

"Lovely to meet you, Layla," Ashton's mother, Clare, said, shaking my hand and smiling at me. "Your dress is so pretty. Where did you get it?" she asked.

"You too. I have heard a lot about you guys. Thank you, my friend let me borrow it for tonight." I looked over at Ashton and found him glaring over at me.

"Good things, I hope," John said, shooting me a wink.

28

"Of course." I was scared that Ashton's parents would be snobby and stuck up, but they didn't seem like it. They seemed really nice and friendly. Nice to know there were nice people in Ashton's family besides him.

"You're the one keeping him in line nowadays," Clare said, smiling over at Ashton affectionately. I looked over at him and found him smiling back at his mom. I loved how he looked at her; his eyes were filled with love and he actually seemed to smile. Feeling really out of place, I knew it was time for me to leave, and because I could feel the bimbo glaring at me.

"Sorry, but I better get back. I have a lot to do," I said politely, smiling at both of them. Sending Ashton a small nod, I turned and left feeling multiple pairs of eyes at my back. *Well, so much for seeing Ashton's reaction to my dress.*

For the next thirty minutes or so, I made rounds saying hi to people and thanking them for coming. I also made sure the waiters were handing out food to guests and that the bartender was doing okay. I saw Neena, Kacey, and Liam talking to people and knew they were fine without me for a while. Checking my phone, I saw it was seven thirty-five and that it was time for Ashton's speech. Excusing myself from a conversation with one of the beneficiaries, I made my way over to Ashton once again. He was in a tight lip-lock battle with his date, and I shoved the hurt I was feeling into the bottom of my heart.

"Mr. Miller," I said, but he didn't seem to hear me. "Mr. Miller!" I said louder, and this time he stopped making out with the blonde and looked at me.

"Yes?" he asked in an annoyed tone.

"You have a speech to make." I tried hard not to sound rude but a little bit slipped out. He sighed and turned to his date.

"I'll be right back, Natasha. Don't move." He sent her a wink and a hard kiss before standing up. I led him to the makeshift stage and stepped back, letting him go up. I let out a sigh and looked out at the crowd as they quieted down, realizing Ashton was about to speak.

"Hello, everyone. Sorry to interrupt your night, but I'd like to say a few things. First off, thank you for coming tonight and making contributions to our cause. I know you all have deep pockets, so don't be afraid to stop and make a contribution before you leave," Ashton joked, and the crowd laughed. I could tell he was in his element. He easily got the guests' attention and flawlessly executed his speech. By the finishing line, people were clapping and almost cheering. I felt proud that I helped with the speech, although I wouldn't be getting any amends for doing so.

He got off the stage and I sent him a smile, but he blew right past me, not even glancing in my direction. I stared after him, forcing myself to get back to work. I couldn't focus on Ashton and his bipolar attitude right now. I lifted up the side of my dress and headed toward my friends. I was almost to them when I suddenly ran into someone. I waited for the feeling of the person's drink to land on me, but nothing happened.

"I am so sorry!" I said, looking up. My gray eyes

clashed with a pair of familiar green eyes. I would know those eyes from anywhere and I instantly froze.

What is he doing here?

I stared into the face that broke my heart for the first time. My ex-boyfriend Jason stood in front of me with the same surprised expression. Never in a million years did I think I would see him again, but here he stood in front of me dressed in a black suit with his blonde hair longer than his old buzz cut.

"Layla?" His deep voice knocked me out of my daze.

"Jason," I said back. How could he be here? I really, really should have looked at the guest list a lot closer! "What are you doing here?" Just staring into those green eyes, I was hit with old memories of us.

"I am here with my company. What are you doing here?" he asked.

"I work at Miller Industries." I had forgotten Jason's family owned Wells Banks. His father was really close to Ashton's father, so of course, he would be here. His father must have stepped down and given Jason his position.

"I'm glad to hear you're doing well," he said almost awkwardly.

"You too. How have your parents been?"

"They've been good. Mom's been busy with the wedding." The moment that left his lips his eyes widened, like he didn't mean for it to slip out.

"Wedding?" I choked out. Great, just another thing to make me feel worse about myself.

"Um, yes. I—" he started to say, but was stopped

when an arm wrapped itself through his own. I looked over and saw a very pretty black-hair girl. I glanced down at her dress and groaned inside my head.

Why is everyone dressed so amazing tonight? And why are all the girls so beautiful that they look like they just stepped out of a magazine?

"Layla, this is my fiancée, Tiffany Gilles. Tiffany, this is one of my old…friends from college, Layla Kingston," Jason said, introducing us. I noticed how he introduced me but I understood. I wouldn't say he was my ex in front of my fiancé either.

"Hi, nice to meet you. Your dress is amazing," I said, shaking her hand and shooting her a semi-fake smile.

"Nice to meet you too. Thanks. Your dress is stunning," she said. Something about her made you like her instantly. She seemed really nice, and I didn't feel jealous at all.

"Oh, thank you." From the corner of my eye, I could sense people were getting kind of agitated. "It was nice meeting you, and nice seeing you again," I said to both of them. "But I have to get going. I'm actually in charge of this gala and have a few things that need to be done. I'm really happy for you guys. You seem perfect for each other." I sent them a wide smile. "If I don't see you guys again, I wish you the best and hope you enjoy the party." With one last goodbye, I quickly walked off.

You handled that pretty well, Layla. I was proud of how I reacted. I could have acted a lot worse, but for some reason seeing Jason here and hearing he was engaged didn't bother me at all. In fact, I was happy for him; he deserved to be happy even after he hurt me. Plus, it was hard to still have feelings for a past boyfriend when your mind was clouded with another person.

Now was not the time to be thinking of past boyfriends and a certain pain in my ass when I had a job to do. I had to make sure all these people didn't get bored and leave early. Heading to the person in charge of the auction, I told him it was time and he went to start it off. As the auction went on, I checked with security, Neena and Kacey, and a few other guests. So far, this night had turned out great; there had only been a few hiccups, and I felt like I had done a good job. While everyone was busy either talking to others or at the auction, I went to the bar and got a drink. I think I deserved one after these past two hectic weeks.

"Can I get a beer?" I asked the bartender. He shot me a surprised look but went and poured me one. I was more of a beer person than a fruity drink one. I really shouldn't be drinking at all, but honestly, could you blame me? I leaned against the bar while looking out at the room, sipping my beer. Everyone seemed to be having a good time, and I smiled. All of this was because of me.

Soon it was almost nine-thirty and the auction was finished, and people seemed a little more relaxed, as they had more drinks in their system. I stayed clear of Ashton and his family, not wanting to be over there and feel Natasha's angry glare at me. I kept tabs on both Neena and Kacey. Neena was with Liam the whole time, and it seemed they were in a deep conversation; anyone could see they liked each other, if only they acted on it. Kacey has been with a tall brown-haired guy since Ashton gave his speech. He looked familiar, but I couldn't remember where I had seen him before. I could see her staring up at him and listening intently to whatever he was saying. Even from here, I could tell she liked him in some way.

As the night wore on, I knew it was time for music. Why have a dance floor if no one would dance? Not wanting to spend money on a band, I found one of the waiters was a DJ as a hobby, so he offered to bring in stuff to play some songs. I just hoped this wouldn't get me in trouble. Going over to the boy, I had him get his stuff ready. Not even a few minutes later, music rang through the room. Heads looked around and I saw a few start to smile. A night full of business talk was boring, and I could tell people were waiting for something fun to start happening.

Ever so slowly, people trickled onto the dance floor. Couples danced with each other, and a few children who had been forced to come with their parents danced around. I grinned as I saw Judy and her husband dancing as well. It was amazing that a couple that had been together since high school were still madly in love. I honestly thought they were the cutest couple in the entire room.

Just then, one of my favorite songs came on. Slowly, everyone who wasn't already dancing grabbed their date's hands and led them onto the dance floor for the slow song. Soon I was literally the only person who wasn't on the dance floor, and the only one without a date it seemed. Even Neena and Kacey were out there with Liam and the mystery guy, and even the few children were dancing, which was actually really cute.

The song started and I stood in the back watching everyone with envy. I had never slow danced with anyone before. I never did when I was with Jason; we just never went anywhere that we could slow dance. I didn't even go to my senior prom or any dance during high school for that matter. Instead, I spent the night with a broken rib, a black eye, and my parents telling me I was too worthless and ugly to have anyone ask me to prom. And my parents were right; no one asked me to prom and no one has ever asked me to dance with them. Dancing in a bar while a few guys pressed against you wasn't considered dancing in my opinion. I guess you could say I was a dance virgin.

My eyes glided over everyone as they danced. Judy and Jack were smiling lovingly at each other, Jason and his fiancée were grinning at each other like love-struck fools, Neena was pressed against Liam, his arm tight around her waist, and with her staring up at him with googly eyes. I felt happy for Neena and hoped Liam would soon ask her out. My eyes next landed on Kacey with her man, and she was laughing at whatever he just said and they each had their arms tight around each other. Staring at them, I realized they seemed to fit each other. Next, I saw Ashton's parents, John and Clare, dancing together. They seemed to be whispering in each other's ears and staring into each other's eyes. My heart ached as I tried to forget I wouldn't have that with someone. Last but not least, my gray eyes landed on Ashton and Natasha.

My heart instantly crumbled at my feet. He was staring down at her with a genuine smile on his face. I knew I had never made him smile like that before and I never would. He twirled her around before drawing her into him. She stared up at him with a big smile and wrapped her arms around his neck. I watched as he acted so carefree and loving toward Natasha. He never once acted like that with me, and my chest ached when a thought suddenly entered my mind. This is who he was supposed to end up with, not someone like me. He needed someone beautiful, confident, model-looking, wealthy, and someone equal to him. I was none of those things. Even in a fairy-like dream dress, I was nothing compared to her; my light not even close to her burning flame. I was like the dirt on the bottom of his shoe he couldn't scrape off.

I watched him and everyone else dance as my heart crumpled into a million pieces. Never in a million years would I get something like that. I will never dance with the love of my life, never will I get the chance to stare into a pair of eyes that would look down at me with so much love in them, never will I be worthy of anyone. My parents had always told me I wouldn't be good enough for anyone, and that if I ever did end up with someone, they would realize I'm not the one and leave me. I believed them, but in this moment, I truly and utterly believed them. They were right. I would always be loveless and worthless.

I sunk against the wall, trying to be invisible as

tears streamed down my face. I had never felt so jealous of everyone than I did in that instant. As the song started to end, I quickly turned and headed to the bathroom. I wiped my face clean so no trace of crying could be seen. Giving myself one pained smile in the mirror, I left the bathroom and headed back to the ballroom. I got there just in time as everyone was heading away from the dance floor. Everyone started leaving and I looked at the clock seeing it was 10:15. I plastered on the fakest smile I have ever put on and turned to her.

"Layla!" I heard Kacey's voice yell my name. I turned and saw her weaving her way toward me. "There you are. I wanted to tell you I'm going to be home late tonight, or maybe tomorrow morning."

"Oh, okay. Where are you going?" I asked.

"Well, do you remember that guy I was with at that club a few weeks ago when you met Ashton?" I thought back to that night and briefly remembered what she was talking about.

"Yeah?"

"That guy is Nick! I didn't know he would be here, and we've been talking all night and even just danced together. He invited me to hang out with him for a few more hours!" she said excitedly. I looked behind her and saw that mystery guy, Nick, staring at us, waiting patiently for Kacey.

"Okay. But be careful, okay? And if you're not coming home, just let me know. I'll be late too," I said, and gave her a quick hug. "He likes you. He can't keep his eyes off of you," I whispered in her ear and pulled away. Her cheeks flushed as she glanced over her shoulder at Nick. "Have fun. And don't do anything I wouldn't!" She shot me a smile and a wink before leaving with Nick.

"Hey," Neena's voice said behind me suddenly. I jumped and gripped my chest.

"Neena, you scared me!"

"Sorry. I just wanted to tell you I'm going to go as well. It was a fun night, and you did a great job tonight," she said, giving me a quick hug.

"Thank you. Let me know when you get home, okay?" I said.

"Well…" She looked down at the ground and I saw a blush creeping onto her cheeks.

"You're not going home."

"Uh, I, um, no. Me and Liam are going to go get a cup of coffee first," she said shyly. I raised an eyebrow, surprised that Neena was embarrassed. She looked up at me and I grinned widely at her.

"Sounds like a date!"

"It is not! It's just two friends getting a cup of coffee together." I just rolled my eyes at her.

"Whatever. You like him and he likes you. It's a date," I said.

"He likes me?" she asked, excitement clear in her voice.

"Duh. He wouldn't have stuck by your side the entire night if he didn't, and he asked you to dance and to get coffee. Plus, he is staring at you right now." Over her shoulder, I could see Liam trying to discreetly look at Neena, not wanting to be caught. I chuckled under my breath before grabbing Neena's shoulders and steering her toward Liam. "Have fun. Use protection, and let me know when you get home safe." With that, I gave her a soft push into

Liam. Winking at both of them, I watched them leave together. Such a cute couple.

I said goodbye to the last few people, relieved I didn't see Ashton again. I don't know if I could have looked at him without bursting into tears. Once all the guests were gone, I slipped off my heels and took a seat in an empty chair. Tonight seemed like a success, and I was glad. I leaned back and closed my eyes, emotionally and physically drained. Glancing around, I saw waiters and the other helpers starting to clean up. The waitress in me knew I had to help, instead of sit here and watch. With that, I stood up, lifting up my dress, and got to work cleaning with the others.

Two hours later, almost everything was cleaned up. The clock struck midnight and I sent everyone home. The rest could be cleaned up tomorrow when I came in, after sleeping in of course. I was exhausted as I grabbed my clutch and slipped back on my heels. I was ready to take off this dress and slip into my regular comfy PJs. My night as a princess was a fail, and I was more than ready to just go home and forget it all. Leaving the building, I locked the door and headed to get a taxi. That was the best thing about New York; you could find a taxi at any time of the day or night. Perks of living in the city that never slept. As I walked down the walkway and onto the street, a heavy hand landed on my shoulder and I let out a scream.

Chapter 4

Layla

As soon as I felt the hand on my shoulder, I let out a scream. Who it could be flashed through my mind in a nanosecond. Was it a homeless person? Was it someone here to rob me? Was it my father? The last thought was the scariest of them all. I was turned around, and my eyes landed on a pair of familiar brown ones.

"Clark, you scared me!" I said, trying to calm my breathing.

"Sorry, Layla," Clark said, his expression actually remorseful.

"What are you doing here?" I asked, changing the subject.

"I am here to drive you home. I figured you would be the last one to leave."

"Oh, thank you, but you didn't have to. Don't you have a family or wife wondering where you are?"

"I already called my wife and told her I would be

home late," he said then gestured to the car. I grabbed the bottom of my dress and slid into the back, I felt bad for making Clark wait for me, but at the same time, I was thankful. As he started the car, I leaned forward in my seat.

"How long have you and your wife been married?" I didn't know anything about Clark apparently.

"We have been together for about fourteen years. We met when we were both twenty. She was in college and I was a fighter." Wow, he didn't look to be in his late thirties.

"One night, after a match, I went to a bar here in New York to blow off some steam. Anyways, I was sitting at a table kind of in the back when this group of ladies walked in. All of them were very beautiful, but my eyes stayed glued to this brown-haired woman with glasses. She looked really out of place dressed in a pair of jeans and a t-shirt while the rest of the girls were wearing tight, short dresses. In my eyes, she was the prettiest of them all. I got the balls to go up and talk to her, and what do you know, she turned me down immediately. After that night, I went back almost every other day to that bar to see her again. It wasn't until a week and a half later that she walked in. I spent that whole night trying to get her attention and for her to say yes to a date. Anyways, long story short, she finally agreed. After dating for almost a year, I proposed to her and for some reason, she said yes and we've been together ever since." The way he talked about her, I knew he loved her with everything he had.

"That is a sweet story," I said, smiling. "She

sounds great."

"She is. She keeps me on my toes." He grinned at me through the review mirror. "Here we are." I looked outside and saw we were outside my apartment.

"Thank you for the ride tonight, Clark." Patting his shoulder, I got out and waved one last time to him before heading inside.

I unlocked my door and pushed through, shutting and locking it behind me. Not bothering to shower since it was so late, I slipped off my dress and placed it gently on a chair in my bedroom. Going into the bathroom, I washed my face free of makeup and pulled out the bobby pins in my hair to pull it up in a bun for bed. After brushing my teeth, I slipped on a pair of comfy PJs, plugged my phone in, and slid under the covers. Tonight made me emotionally drained, and I was ready to be pulled into sleep and forget it all.

Laying my head on my pillow, I tried to fall asleep. You would think since I hadn't slept much in the last two weeks I would immediately fall asleep, but instead, I tossed and turned, trying to get a certain person's face out of my head.

***

The next morning, I got up around nine-thirty or so. I laid in bed staring up at the ceiling, debating if I really needed to get up today. I just wanted to stay in bed all day and read my book or something. After having an internal debate for about fifteen minutes, I finally got up and got in the shower. Washing off all of last night, I got out feeling clean and refreshed. All I planned on doing today was finish cleaning up the venue from last night then coming back home to eat junk food and watch tv. I slipped on a pair of yoga pants, a sports bra, and a tank top. Piling my hair into a ponytail, I left my bedroom to grab something quick to eat then I was ready to go. The sooner I left, the sooner I could get back home.

Grabbing a random yogurt from the fridge, I glanced around and knew Kacey wasn't home. *Probably spent the night with Nick,* I thought. I slipped on a pair of flip flops, grabbed my things, and left the apartment. I didn't care if I didn't match or if I was wearing workout clothes. It wasn't like I was going to be seeing anyone while I was cleaning. I got a taxi pretty quick and was soon headed to The Smith Center.

Walking through the door, I couldn't help but think about last night. Instead of feeling sorry for myself, I decided I was going to put a wall around my heart and that way it wouldn't get hurt again. I was tired of feeling sad and angry at Ashton. If he wanted to act like a jackass, then so be it. I wasn't going to show him that he had hurt me. With a new feeling of confidence, I got to work cleaning up the rest from last night.

I was thankful that I had thought ahead of time for the cleaning part. I hired some cleaning crew to take care of the decorations, and to clean the floors. Then I got someone to come by and pick up the plates, glasses, and silverware to take back to the shop. All I had to do was make sure the donations were picked up this morning and that no one left anything. Last night, I had helped throw away extra food and clean the tables off. I was in the middle of stacking up plates and putting them in a box so the people could take them when a deep velvety voice called my name behind me. I steeled myself and turned toward him.

"Mr. Miller," I said, keeping any emotion out of my voice. What was Ashton even doing here?

"I figured you would be here," Ashton said, coming toward me. He looked different today. Instead of wearing his usual work attire, he was wearing a pair of dark blue jeans and a fitted gray t-shirt. If I thought Ashton in a suit was hot, this was even hotter. Casual Ashton was H-O-T! Pulling my gaze away from his body, I looked over his shoulder at the wall, not wanting to make eye contact. I knew if I did the wall around my heart would crumble faster than the Berlin Wall.

"Yes, I am. Why are you here?" I asked, my voice clipped.

"I wanted to talk to you about last night."

"And you couldn't have used the phone?"

"No, I wanted to talk face-to-face."

"Then go ahead, I have things that need to be done," I said. He was quiet for a few minutes and I felt him looking me up and down. Everywhere his eyes looked seemed to burn like his eyes were lasers cutting my clothes off.

"Last night was…okay," Ashton said, breaking the silence. I clenched my jaw and finally looked at him.

"Just 'okay?'"

"Yes, it could have been better. But since you are

new to this, I will let it slide." He spoke in a nonchalant way. My hands unconsciously curled into fists. I wanted to pound on his face until he acted differently. "I have a few things for you to do before Monday," he said.

"Sorry, I have plans," I lied. No way in hell was I working on a Saturday, especially after what I had to do last night. "It will have to wait until Monday." He narrowed his eyes at me.

"What plans?" he asked, his voice low.

"None of your business. Now is that all?" When he didn't answer, I brushed past him ignoring his burning gaze on my backside. I opened my phone and dialed Kacey's number, silently fuming at Ashton.

"Hello?" Kacey answered, her voice thick with sleep.

"Kacey, we are going out tonight." I then said something I had never said in all of my twenty-three years of life. "I want to get drunk."

***

Ashton

I watched Layla walk off and couldn't help but stare at her ass encased in those damn yoga pants. *She needs to wear those more often,* I thought. I momentarily forgot why I was mad at her as she stalked away from me. *Where is she going tonight?* I couldn't help but ask myself. I knew it was none of my business, but I didn't want Layla going on a date with some guy or anyone for that matter. I growled under my breath and tromped to my car outside.

Layla had every right to be pissed at me, especially with how I acted last night and just a few moments ago. I lied when I said the gala was just okay; it was honestly great! Everything went and looked perfect. In all the galas that had been thrown in the last couple of years, this one was the best of them all. All night, people had come over to me and told me they loved the decorations and everything about the party. They asked me who did it, but I didn't tell them it was Layla and I felt bad that I didn't. She did an amazing job, and I felt guilty that I didn't have anyone help her. It was a dick move and I realize that now.

I didn't know what I was trying to do to her. Maybe get her to quit so I wouldn't have to see her every day and want to go over to her and kiss her senseless every second of every day. Everything I did last night, I regretted. I shouldn't have brought Natasha with me, and I shouldn't have ignored Layla the entire night, especially when she was just doing the job I told her to do. All night I couldn't keep my eyes off of her. In that stunning red dress, she looked irresistible and I had to hold back a growl every time I saw another man look at her with lust. That dress hugged her curves perfectly and made her skin look tan. It took every part of my being to not go over there and take her somewhere to ravish her. The more I looked at Layla, the angrier I got at myself. Trying to distract myself from her, I would kiss Natasha or hold her tightly against me, but in the back of my mind instead of seeing Natasha's face, I saw Layla's.

I would never tell anyone, but when I walked into the room with Natasha on my arm, I looked over at Layla and saw her face. Her expression almost brought me to my knees. There was no mistaking the hurt in her eyes or the sadness that passed across her face. I knew she picked out my suit for me and I purposely wore it. The voice in my head told me I shouldn't, but knowing that Layla handpicked it, I felt the need to wear it. It was the closest way to be with her and not be with her. When Layla came over to meet my parents last night, I clenched Natasha hard against me. The smell of Layla's perfume was intoxicating, and I tightened my jaw so I would lean in and smell her as she greeted my parents with a smile.

The moment Layla walked away, I let out a breath I didn't know I was holding. My mom then went on about how she liked Layla and approved of her. My mother didn't easily accept people—hell, she hated Natasha's guts—but in just a few moments, Layla had my mother's approval. The moment I regretted the most, though, was when I kissed Natasha in front of Layla. I didn't miss the hurt look on her face, and I instantly wanted to rewind the last minute and not kiss Natasha but Layla instead. Hell, if I were rewinding I would rewind to the moment I broke it off with Layla and have her as my date instead.

I was being an utter dick to her, but I knew that pushing her away was easier so I wouldn't hurt her. *But you're already hurting her in the process.* Before leaving the party last night, I snuck a quick glance at Layla one last time and saw her talking to her friend. From here I could see her smile and I knew it wasn't a real one. Her friend didn't seem to notice the act Layla was putting on, but I could. When I got in the car behind Natasha, my mind was elsewhere as Clark drove us away from The Smith Center, away from Layla. Instead of taking Natasha to my place and sleeping with her, I had Clark drop her off at the hotel she had been staying at over the past few weeks. She was leaving tomorrow.

She clearly didn't understand why I wasn't going to sleep with her and kept asking me why we were here instead of at my place, but I just dismissed her. I told her I was tired and for her to get out. Not even glancing her way, I heard her huff and slam the car door behind her. Telling Clark to take me home, I leaned back in the seat suddenly feeling tired. Once we pulled up, I got out and told Clark to wait for Layla at the venue to take her home. With that, I went inside and went into my office. I gripped my head and thought about Layla the rest of the night.

***

Layla

After ending the call with Kacey, I had called Neena and told her we were going out and to be at my place by seven. I had spent the rest of the morning and afternoon calling the cleaning service, and cleaning my own apartment to waste time until both of my friends came over and we got ready. I was never one to really drink and go out and party, but I needed to. I needed to relax and forget about everything. Hell, I deserved it. When Kacey came home around four or five, I turned the tables and questioned her about her night with Nick.

I then spent the next hour and a half learning about him. He apparently owned his own business in technology, he was also a millionaire like Ashton, and I, unfortunately, found out he was Ashton's best friend. I let that part go, for now, and let Kacey continue to tell me how sweet and caring Nick was. I only partly listened to her; I was a terrible friend. I made comments in the right spots and nodded when needed. Finally, it was seven and Neena knocked on the door right on time. I let her in and she instantly started asking me why I wanted to go out clubbing.

"Stupid Ashton. That's all I'm going to say," I said, waving the rest of their questions off. Luckily both of them were just happy I wanted to go out tonight, and were supportive enough to come out with me.

We got ready together, and I had to borrow another outfit from Kay. *I really need to go shopping soon,* I thought as I pulled on a skintight dress that Kacey handed me. It was a pretty blue color and ended about mid-thigh. Since I had pulled my hair up in a bun this morning while it was still wet, it dried wavy. Kacey just added a little mousse in it, and the waves looked almost beachy. My makeup was light, and my eyeshadow matched the blue in my dress. I borrowed a pair of heels that matched the dress from Kay's closet, while she flat-ironed Neena's hair.

"So, Neena, how was last night with Liam?" I asked out of the blue, waiting for Kacey to finish her own makeup. I could see Neena blushing as she turned away from me.

"Ohhh, something happened!" Kacey said, grabbing her dress.

"Did not! We didn't do anything," Neena said defensively, but she didn't sound too convincing.

"Yeah, we don't believe that," I said, smiling at her. "Come on, tell us!"

"Fine." She sighed. "We went and got coffee after the gala. Instead of taking a taxi home, Liam walked me home and we looked at the stars and just talked. We got to know each other and when he dropped me off at home, we…kissed." I turned to Kacey, and we both grinned.

"Aw! Neena, you like him a lot, don't you?" I said. She talked about him in a dreamy voice. When she didn't say anything, my grin got wider.

"Oh, would you look at that? It's eight-thirty already. We better get going," Neena said and got up, leaving the room. Both Kacey and I chuckled and followed after her. Yup, she liked him, and by her actions, I could tell it was a lot.

We got to the same club where I met Ashton about twenty minutes later. The club was already packed, and it was only nine. Since Kacey knew the bouncer up front, we were able to bypass the long line and get inside. We ignored the angry protests of the people waiting in the line, and thanked the bouncer. The moment we stepped inside, I was slammed with the bass of the music. We pushed through the masses of sweaty bodies until we reached the bar.

"Six shots of tequila!" Kacey yelled over the music at the cute bartender. He set the six in front of us and sent us a wink before leaving to help other customers. Neena raised an eyebrow at us since we weren't IDed, but we just shrugged.

"Here you go." Kacey handed us two shot glasses each. They weren't the small shot glasses either; they were big and probably held two regular shots in just the one.

"Here's to Layla for getting drunk for only the second time in her life, and to ignoring that asshole Ashton Miller!" I smiled and cheered them both before tossing back the first shot then quickly the second one. It burnt the whole way down my throat, and my eyes and nose burnt. I bit back the cough that was making its way up my throat. That was some strong tequila.

"Woo!" Neena yelled, setting her shots down. "Let's go dancing!" I barely set down my shot glasses before I was pulled by both Kacey and Neena onto the dance floor. I let the music weave itself around me and I started to relax. The shots were starting to take effect, and my hips were moving on their own. A Jason Derulo song came on, and I put my hands in the air and moved my hips. I danced with Neena and Kacey, smiling and laughing. For the first time in a long time, I relaxed and let myself have a good time.

We danced through six or so songs until I shouted to them that we should get more shots. When they nodded in agreement, I laced my arms through theirs and pulled us back to the bar. My skin was sweaty and my hair was sticking to my face and neck.

"Three tequila shots!" I yelled to the same bartender.

"Here you sexy ladies go," he said, smiling at me. I grinned back before handing Kay and Neena their shots. "Bottoms up!" With that, I took the shot and slammed it back down on the bar.

"One more!" Neena yelled.

"No, no, I don't think we should," I said. I was already feeling the other three.

"Nope, you are having one more," Kay said, and handed me another one. I took a breath and cheered with them before shooting it. The burn wasn't as bad as before. Grinning widely, I made my way back to the dance floor when one of my favorite songs came on. Usher's "Yeah" came on, and I almost yelled.

"I love this song!" I yelled at them both. This was my weakness. Everyone has a stripper song, and this one was mine. I was moving my hips, moving my hands in the air, and closing my eyes when I felt a big hand wrap itself around my waist. I opened my eyes and turned to see who was grabbing me. A pretty good-looking guy was dancing behind me.

"You sure know how to dance," he said into my ear. I could feel him grinding himself on my backside and I moved away. I wasn't here to get it on with some random guy.

"Thanks, but I'm not interested," I said, pulling away from him. Before he could protest, I saw Neena and Kacey and moved toward them.

We danced for a while, and I felt the alcohol starting to really affect me. I staggered a little in my heels and my head was kind of foggy. I was slurring my words, and my body felt hot. Kacey and Neena were pretty far off like I was.

"I think…we should go," I said to both of them. It was getting kind of late. They nodded, and we staggered through the dance floor and out the front door.

"Ladies, do you need a taxi?" the bouncer asked. I think I nodded, but I wasn't so sure. A minute later, the bouncer was helping us get in the taxi. We were all giggling like little girls when we squeezed into the back.

"Where to, ladies?" the taxi driver asked. I stared at him trying to think of the address.

"144 Hilton Drive," I said to him. He nodded and started forward. The whole way, us three were slurring at one another and laughing at stupid things.

"We are here," the taxi driver said.

"Thank you. Girls…me stay here. Go home," I said and told the driver my real address. The girls were too far gone to realize what I said. He looked at me weird, but I was already out of the cab and walking to the front doors. The cool night air seemed to clear my head only slightly. I stared up at the building and stumbled in. I got to the elevator and hit the floor I wanted. I leaned against the wall of the elevator and licked my dry lips. I pulled my sweaty hair to the side of my shoulder and staggered out when the doors opened. I made my way to the right door and knocked loudly. I kept knocking and gripped the corner of the doorframe so I wouldn't fall. Suddenly, the door opened but my hand was already moving forward. Instead of my hand hitting the door, I hit a hard chest.

"Layla?" someone asked. I looked up into the face of Ashton. He was staring down at me, confused.

"Ashton!" I called out.

"What are you wearing?" he asked, looking down at my outfit. The material had ridden up some and was showing more of my legs.

"A pretty dress." I giggled. I reached out and touched his cheek with my hand. "So pretty," I cooed.

"You are drunk," Ashton said.

"I am not!" I glanced around and leaned in closer to him. "That's a lie. I am so drunk," I whispered to him. Ashton sighed and grabbed my arm and pulled me into his apartment. I honestly had no idea why I came here, but it was too late to go anywhere else.

"Layla, why are you drunk?" Ashton talked down to me.

"You cause this!" I blurted out.

"Me?"

"Yes, you sexy man." Man, this alcohol was making me very confident. "I wouldn't be drunk if I didn't have to deal with you and your annoyingness."

"Annoyingness?"

"Yes, you know what I am talking about. You...you...you...nutbottom!" I staggered in my heels and leaned against Ashton. With a grunt, I leaned down and slid out of my heels. I let out a

54

moan and threw my shoes.

"Layla, let's go get you some water," Ashton said, gently holding onto my elbow and my lower back guiding me toward the kitchen.

"Why are you so hot and rude all the time?" I blabbed. *Mouth, shut up!* I yelled at myself internally. "You would be a lot sexier if you weren't so, so, so…" I flapped my arms around trying to find the word. "Polar!" I yelled a second later.

"Bipolar, you mean?" Ashton said, pulling a bar chair out for me. He grabbed my hips and set me down on it.

"Yes! You and I were always so," I said, putting my hand by my forehead and gesturing between us.

"I think I like drunk Layla." Ashton grinned at me as he got a glass and filled it with ice-cold water.

"No, you don't like me. You told me you hate me," I whined. *Wow, sudden mood twist.* "I'm just too good for you." Smiling at that thought, I laughed at Ashton.

"I don't hate you, Layla," he said, grabbing my hand and putting the cold cup in it. Afraid I would drop it, he helped guide it to my lips. I gulped down the water in seconds before pulling away and smacking my lips.

"Water is sooooooo good. Why does it taste so good?" I asked. My head rolled to the side as Ashton got me more water.

"Why were you out drinking?" He changed the subject. I was too drunk to really notice.

I started singing to Katy Perry's "Hot N Cold", but stopped a minute later, forgetting the words.

"Nothing I do is right, just like with my parents. I thought when I moved away I could get away from all the negative shit but no."

Ashton handed me the water and I took a sip.

"I'm almost back where I was, but at least there's no hitting this time," I said, looking around and unaware of what I said. "I love the color here." My mind changed the subject.

"Wait, Layla, hitting?" Ashton asked, getting in front of me. I stayed silent for a few minutes.

"I'm tired!" I whined. "Take me to bed, oh noble one!" I held out my arms to Ashton and giggled. He stared at me, but finally sighed before helping me off the chair. When my feet hit the ground, I jumped on him and wrapped my arms around him like a koala bear. "I'm a koala bear!" Tequila really made me confident and loud.

"Are you going to get off of me?"

"Nope!" I said, popping the "p". He shook his head but started walking toward his room. I started slipping, so I moved up Ashton's body until my arms were wrapped tight around his neck and my legs were around his waist. His arms snaked around me and gripped me against him. I laid my head on his shoulder and felt my eyelids starting to droop.

"Me sleepy," I mumbled. Somehow, he carried me up the stairs and to his bed.

"Let's get you out of this dress than you can sleep," he said. Feeling suddenly tired, I felt his fingers reaching for the zipper. He unzipped me and shimmied the dress down my chest, waist, and finally to pool at my feet. His face was in line with my stomach, and I briefly heard his intake of breath.

The moment his fingers touched the scar on my stomach, my skin zinged and I jumped.

"Where did you get this?" Ashton questioned, his voice quiet. I looked down at him with hooded eyes.

"Nowhere," I mumbled, gripping his shoulders as I wobbled. I wasn't concerned at all that I was only in a strapless bra and panties. He asked again.

"I don't want to talk about it right now."

He looked up at me and searched my face. He finally let it go and stood up. Going over to his walk-in closet, he came back out with a t-shirt and boxers. He gently lifted up my arms and put my arms through the holes. He knelt down and helped me put my feet through the boxers with my hands on his shoulders. I was surprisingly quiet, as was he.

"There you go," he said quietly. My eyelids were getting heavy and I was getting sleepier. "Come lie down." Ashton helped me on the bed and he pulled the covers back. Once I was settled in, he tucked me in and kissed my forehead. "Get some sleep, Layla. I'll see you in the morning." I smiled as my eyes closed and I was lulled to sleep.

**

Ashton

I stood over Layla's sleeping form and sighed. I hadn't expected Layla to show up so late, and drunk at that. It was surprising, but I was glad. Being around her drunk was hilarious, but they say when you're drunk, the real you comes out. As she slept, I thought back to the big scar on her stomach. It looked terrible and only a few years old. What she said earlier about being hit and now seeing that scar, I was starting to piece things together. How could someone do that to her?

When she snuggled deeper into the bed and pillow, my heart yearned for her. The feeling to protect her got bigger, and I couldn't help but want to be with her. Shaking my head at myself, I stripped out of my clothes until I was in my boxers and climbed into the other side of the bed. I reached out and pulled Layla to me. She snuggled back against me and I smiled. With her body pressed to mine, I slowly fell asleep.

Chapter 5

Layla

I woke up the next morning with a pounding headache. It felt like someone was playing the drums right next to my head. I groaned and curled deeper into the comfy bed, bringing my hands up to hold my head. *And this is why I don't get drunk.* The last time I did, it was so bad I vowed to never go it again. Thankfully, this time I didn't throw up. *Oh, wait? Did I?* I questioned. I waved it off and snuggled into the bed wrapping the thick cover around myself.

Breathing in deeply, I smelled a mix of lavender and something else familiar. It smelled like a mix of cologne and man. With my eyes still closed, I rolled over and sniffed the bed, smelling the scent stronger here. I knew I looked like a weirdo, but I couldn't stop myself from smelling the bed and the intoxicating scent. Whatever it was I wanted to put it in a container and keep it. *What is wrong with you today, Layla?* It was weird that I had this kind of

59

manly scent on my bed, but I didn't question it. For some strange reason, the longer I smelt the bed, my headache seemed to go away.

I was starting to wake up and as I slowly started to gain consciousness, I could hear footsteps heading toward my room. As they got closer, I groaned loudly.

"Kay, how much did we drink last night?" I asked from under the covers. "My head is pounding." Kacey didn't answer, but I heard her moving around the room. The longer she didn't reply, the suspicious I became. "Kacey?" I said her name again, but the same thing happened. Confused, I pulled the covers away from my face and peeked out. The sun hit my eyes and I hissed, putting my hand over my eyes. *Okay, yes, I am never drinking again!* After a minute, I was okay and let my hand fall. I glanced around and sat up with a gasp. This was not my room.

My eyes moved to the right and I saw Ashton standing there pulling on a white T-shirt. *How the hell did I get here?*

"A-Ashton?" I squeaked out. He turned around at the sound of my voice.

"You're awake, good." He came toward the bed and sat on the edge a little bit away from me.

"What am I doing here?" I asked, glancing around. I swallowed, my mouth feeling like cotton.

"You showed up here last night around eleven or so, drunk," Ashton said, shrugging before standing up and walking toward his bathroom. He returned a minute later with a glass of water.

"Here you go. This should help with the

headache." He handed me a glass of water and some Advil. I quickly took the pills and swallowed them.

"I don't remember coming here," I muttered, holding the now-empty glass on my lap. When I had moved to grab the glass, the bedspread had moved off of me, I looked down and saw my bare legs and then a pair of what looked to be boxers. "Did you undress me?"

"I did. But I didn't peek, if that's what you're wondering," Ashton replied. That wasn't what I was worried about. I was worried that he saw my scars and would start asking me about them. Seeing as he didn't say anything else after that, I figured he wasn't going to say anything about them, or at least not yet anyways.

"Oh god, please tell me I didn't do anything stupid last night," I said, moving to cover my face as I thought about everything that I could have done.

"Nothing too extreme," Ashton said with amusement. "But I got to say, drunk Layla is my new favorite person." He shot me a smirk and then backed away. "I have breakfast downstairs waiting for you. Come down in a minute." Just the thought of food made my stomach heave.

"No, I don't think I can eat right now," I said turning green.

"You have to. If not, your hangover is going to be way worse." Not waiting for my reply, he turned and left the room. I groaned and fell back on the bed. I didn't feel like moving at all. I knew if I didn't go down there in just a few minutes then Ashton would have no problem coming back up here to bring me down with him. With another loud groan, I swung my legs off the bed and stood up. As I did so, the room started to spin. I quickly closed my eyes and held my head.

Stupid fucking alcohol. I cursed in my head.

After standing like that for a good three minutes, I opened my eyes and thankfully the room wasn't spinning anymore. With somewhat shaky legs, I slowly made my way downstairs, holding the banister as I went. Just as I made it down the stairs, Ashton walked out of the kitchen like he was coming to get me.

"There you are. Come." I walked behind him into the kitchen and resisted the urge to throw up as the smell of food hit my nose. I slumped down onto a stool and shivered. My bare feet hit the metal of the chair. "Just a few bites," Ashton said once he saw the look on my face.

"I am never drinking again," I said as he put a plate in front of me. On it was a plain piece of toast, a few eggs, and a piece of bacon, as well as a big glass of orange juice.

"That's what you say now," he joked before taking a seat next to me with a plate piled with food. I watched him eat and pushed the food around on my plate. "Layla, eat. Now," he ordered. Sighing, I picked up the plain toast and nibbled on it. Ashton nodded as he watched me eat as he ate as well.

We ate in silence, and soon my stomach settled down and I was able to everything on my plate. The silence wasn't awkward, but I was aware of everything Ashton did. After I was done, I got up and went to wash my plate. Even though I wasn't the biggest fan of him right now, I wasn't going to make him clean up after me. As I started cleaning my plate, I could feel Ashton's eyes on me and I tried not to squirm under his gaze. The way he stared at me was like he was staring into my soul or something.

"So those were your plans last night. Getting drunk?" he asked, breaking the silence.

"Maybe," I answered, putting my plate in his dishwasher. I held my hand out for his plate and he put it in my open hand.

"Getting drunk and grinding with horny guys is much more important than your job, huh?" His voice was getting hard and angry. "And you were by yourself. Don't you know how dangerous that is? Don't you remember me saving you last time you went partying?" He was now standing up and practically yelling at me. The plate in my hand now forgotten as I glared at him.

"I was not alone; I had my friends. And why do you care?" I yelled back at him. "Two weeks ago, you didn't give a flying shit what happened to me."

"I care if my PA is found dead on the street."

"Nice to know how much I mean to you. All you fucking care about is work and yourself! Do you know how frustrating you are? One second you are sweet and caring, then the next you're cold and being a jackass. You don't care about other people's feelings. You make me run all over town and do all different kinds of shit at the office and I don't even get a 'thank you.' You dropped this whole gala thing on me and I had to do it by *myself*! Then you had the balls to tell me it was 'just okay!'"

"I told you that this job had to be taken seriously and that you would be at my beck and call. So, don't stand there telling me what I am giving you is shit. You are lucky I even gave you a job!" He seethed at me. His blue eyes were hard and narrowed at me.

"I am not yelling at you about work. I am trying to tell you I am sick and tired of you acting like such an ass to me. You were the one who ended it, not me! I should be the one pissed at you instead of the other way around."

"You want me to treat you nice? Sorry, princess, but I treat all my other mistakes the same way." His cruel words cut into me. I sucked in a breath and stumbled back like he had hit me. *A mistake.* I would always be the mistake. Clenching my jaw tightly, I gave Ashton my deadliest glares.

"I am done with you, Ashton. I am done with you putting me down and making this my fault when it is your own damn fault. I want *nothing* to do with you outside of work. The only reason I will continue to work for you is just what you said: I need it. At work, I will do as you ask but nothing more. You don't have to worry about this *mistake* anymore." I moved passed him and made it to the kitchen doorway before turning back to him. "Sorry you ever had to look at this ugly face or ever touch me. Hope you have more fun with Natasha," I said venomously. With that, I left the kitchen. On a table by the door were my dress and heels from last night. Picking them up, I threw open the door and slammed it shut behind me.

As I made my way downstairs, ignoring all the

curious glances being thrown at me, I hailed a cab. I knew I looked like a hurricane had hit me. I bet my hair was everywhere, and I knew I looked ridiculous wearing a huge t-shirt, a pair of boxer briefs, and blue high heels, but I didn't care. Right now, I was too angry and hurt to care.

I made it home in no time and stomped up the stairs to my apartment. Throwing open the door, I slammed it behind me and walked to my room. My body was shaking, but I didn't know if it was because of how angry I was or because sobs were trying to break free. I heard Kacey's snores down the hall, but I slammed my door shut, not caring. And for what seemed for the hundredth time, I fell on my bed crying because of a certain asshole.

***

I spent most of Sunday barricaded in my room, not answering any of Kacey or Neena's bangs. Why the hell did I think it was a good idea going to Ashton's house last night? And why did I have a feeling of hopefulness in my stomach when I woke up and saw him? I knew everything about Ashton was bad. I shouldn't have agreed to this job, going on a date with him, and I shouldn't have done anything with him in the first place. When I saw him for the first time, I knew he was trouble but me being me, I didn't listen to my head. And boy, did I regret it now.

Everything I said to him I meant. I was tired of being clobbered by him. I would keep working there until I could find another job, but while I looked I would be stuck being Ashton's PA. In the back of my mind, I had hoped that maybe Ashton would apologize and we would kind of go back to whatever we were, but now I knew we didn't have a chance to fully become a couple. I was too broken and Ashton was too selfish. I knew somehow Ashton had gotten hurt pretty badly if he turned out the way he is now. They say opposites attract, but in our case, we didn't.

When the clock was a little past noon, I decided to get up and leave my room. I had heard Kacey and Neena leave a few hours before, so I didn't have to worry about being interrogated by them. God knew that if I did, I would be back to crying once again. For the moment, I was fine. I padded into my small kitchen in my mismatched socks and opened the fridge. It looked practically empty, as were the cabinets I opened up a second later. Sighing, I knew I had to run to the grocery store.

I dressed in another pair of yoga pants, stolen from Kacey, a white V-neck, and a pair of flip flops. I pulled my messy hair into a bun at the top of my head, grabbed my stuff, then left the house. I didn't care what I looked like; this was New York. There were plenty of weird people walking about for me to go unnoticed. The closest grocery-like store we had was a few blocks down. It was more of a Whole Foods than anything else; thankfully, though, it was cheaper than Whole Foods.

I walked the few blocks and breathed in the warm air and sighed. Being outside could do wonders for someone's health. I could feel my body relaxing and my head clearing. It seemed all I needed was to get out for a little bit. Passing through the doors of the store, I grabbed a handbasket and started my shopping. I walked every aisle, taking my time since I had nowhere to be today. I didn't have a list, so I just threw stuff in the basket that we usually get and looked good. The store was pretty busy and I had to navigate through it.

As I turned a corner to go to a different aisle, I ran right into someone. My basket dropped, and I almost fell but a pair of arms gripped my forearms, pulling me forward and into a hard chest.

"I am so sorry!" I said, looking up. Staring down at me was a pretty pair of green eyes. My breath got stuck in my throat as I took in the rest of the man's face. He had well-defined cheek bones and jawline. His blonde hair was tousled on top of his head in a messy just-got-out-of-bed way. There was a little bit of scruff on his chin and jaw that made him look very sexy. He stood about six-foot-two, and I could tell he had a great body underneath that tight shirt. Whoever this guy was, he was very hot!

"No, I am sorry. I should have been watching where I was going." The sound of his deep, smooth voice entered my ears, and I jerked out of my gawking. I could feel a blush starting to spread on my cheeks.

"It was my fault," I said, stepping out of his hold. He was wearing a dark gray quarter-sleeve shirt, and a pair of dark grayish-blue jeans; he also had a pair of Converse on. He squatted down and grabbed the few items that had fallen out of my basket and then handed it to me.

"Here you go," he said, shooting me a gorgeous smile. My knees felt weak and my arms like Jell-O. "Sorry for running into you…"

"I'm Layla."

"Sorry for running into you, Layla." The way he said my name, I almost melted. *Good god, he is unbelievably attractive.*

"I am too…"

"Alex." I smiled at him. Alex definitely suited him for some reason.

"Are you here shopping by yourself?" he asked, picking up his own hand basket.

"Yeah, I am." I nodded. "I'm just picking up some food for me and my roommate since our fridge is practically empty," I said with a nervous laugh.

"Mind if I join you then?" My throat was suddenly dry, so I just nodded. I walked down the aisle beside him, trying to think of something to say that wouldn't make me look like an idiot.

"I take it you live around here?" Alex thankfully asked first.

"Yeah. I live a few blocks down the road. How about you?" I asked, turning my head and looking up at him. I could see his arm muscles through his shirt as he held his basket.

"Yeah, kind of. I live a little bit further from here, but I like this store so I make the trip here."

"Ahh, so this is your dating pool, huh?" I joked, sending him a teasing smile. After only meeting him three minutes ago, I felt comfortable around him. He seemed nice and sweet.

"Of course. See that lady in the purple shirt?" He

pointed to an older lady who looked to be in her late sixties. "She's a fox in the bed. Watch out for her." I let out a loud laugh that made a lot of people to look at us. I slapped a hand over my mouth, muffling my laughter.

"You have a cute laugh," Alex said, smiling down at me. I forced the blush down that was threatening to break free.

"Thank you," I said quietly

We walked down the rest of the aisles, not saying much. I felt comfortable in Alex's presence. He seemed so sweet and funny. The total opposite of Ashton. The moment I thought his name, I pushed it away. I was not going to think or compare anyone to Ashton. Way too soon, we came to a stop at a register. Alex let me go first, and I put my basket on top of the conveyer belt. I realized I only grabbed a few things and when I bumped into Alex, I didn't grab anything else.

From the corner of my eye, I saw him put his basket behind mine. I couldn't deny my attraction to him. He was by far one of the hottest guys I had ever seen. I could feel myself getting my hopes up that he would ask me for my number or something. As the lady rang up my items, I couldn't help but chide myself. How stupid was I to be pining after another guy when just this morning I was at Ashton's house and crying over him. You would think by now I would give up on guys, but here I was, flirting with another at the grocery store.

"That will be twenty-eight dollars and fifty cents," the cashier said. I reached into my bag and fished out my wallet. Just as I was pulling out two twenties, a hand shoved theirs in front of mine and toward the lady. I looked over and saw Alex smiling at the lady while handing her money.

"Alex?" I hissed out.

"What?" He shrugged innocently at me, grabbing the change the lady gave to him.

"You shouldn't have paid for my groceries," I said. I didn't know this man, but here he was paying for my stuff.

"It's no big deal," he said then softly nudged me to move over, as his stuff was being rang through. I moved the two bags I had off to the side and stared at the side of Alex's face. "You know a picture would last longer," he teased, shooting me a smirk. *God, even his smirk is sexy.* I tried to muster a comeback, but he left me flustered. Once he was done paying, he grabbed his bags and waited for me to go ahead of him.

I grunted and walked ahead of his out the doors. When I got outside, I turned to him.

"Alex, let me pay you back," I said, but he cut me off.

"Don't. Layla, it is no big deal. It's the least I could do after running into you earlier."

"But I ran into you. I don't want you to waste your money on me," I argued. He just stood in front of me, staring me down. Feeling his jade eyes on me, I finally sighed. "Fine, but let me pay you back somehow."

"How about you let me take you out on a date," Alex said.

"How is that *me* paying *you* back?" I questioned him.

"I get to be in your lovely company again." He grinned. I couldn't help but laugh quietly and shake my head. All different kinds of questions entered my mind as I thought about my answer. *You know what? For the first time, I am not going to question it. I am going to go for it.*

"Okay, yes," I answered, grinning back at him. His smile somehow got wider as he put his bags in one big hand. He reached his hand in the pocket of his jeans and pulled out his phone. He tapped on it for a second before handing it to me.

"Give me your number." I took his phone and entered it in. "I'll send you a text so you have my number." I nodded, feeling giddy. I just got a hot guy's phone number! Inside I was freaking out, but on the outside, I tried not to do anything stupid. "I'll call you and set up a date, if that's okay."

"Sounds good."

"It was nice meeting you, Layla. I'm glad I ran into you," Alex said.

"Me too." I sent him a small wave as we both turned in opposite directions. As I walked away, I couldn't help but look over my shoulder after him. He was looking over his shoulder at me as well, sending me a goofy smile. I grinned widely as I turned back around and headed home. My phone buzzed in my bag, so I stopped, shifting my bags around before grabbing my phone.

From: Unknown
To: Layla
Watch out for any more of my foxy ladies at the store. ;)

71

I laughed and shook my head as I walked home. Who knew this day would start out so shitty but ended up so good? And who knew I would meet such a nice guy at the grocery store?

Chapter 6

Layla

There is a quote that I have always been fascinated and stumped with: "Sometimes, when finding the light, you have to pass through the deepest darkness." You have to suffer before you can see the rainbow. You have to suffer heartbreaks before it can fully heal and be fully loved. I'd always wondered why people choose to do this to themselves. Why put your heart out there if it's just going to break? Why do us humans purposely do this to ourselves? Do we like the pain? Do we actually think that after our suffering a rainbow will appear?

When you think about it, though, the analogy is fitting. After a terrible storm, where the winds have knocked down branches, rain coming down in sheets so that the roads flood, and thunder booms so loudly the windows rattle. After all that is over, if you look to the sky, you see a rainbow in the aftermath of the storm. Rain softly falls and the clouds part, showing a full rainbow to anyone who dares to go outside. In those moments, there is nothing but silence. No birds chirping, no loud booms of thunder, no brutal wind—just utter silence.

If you dare to go outside after the storm, you can almost see the beauty in it. The roads glistening, the sky turning the perfect shade of blue, the dead silence with no wind whipping in your face. In those moments, you forget that just minutes ago a storm was whipping its way through town and destroying almost everything in its path. How can something so beautiful come out of so much destruction? Is that how a heart looks after a heartbreak?

But like every storm, there is the aftermath; the clean-up. When something gets broken or destroyed it needs to be fixed. Does it get fixed perfectly? No. Does it change the shape or reconfiguring? Yes. When something gets broken, it's not expected to turn out perfect again or even close to what it used to be. Whether it can be fixed to be even stronger than before, or if it will crumble easier is the question. The difference between a storm and a broken heart is *you* get to decide whether your heart will be stronger than it was, or to be weaker.

In college, I took a psychology class and I'd never been so interested in a class before. The professor once said that there are two types of people when dealing with heartache or loss. One will act out and walks around with an almost visible shield around themselves. The other one becomes secluded and walks around with their heart showing. One heart has been healed crooked and becomes weaker, so a shield needs to be put in place; they don't see the rainbow at the end. The other has been healed slowly but carefully; it's stronger than it once was and doesn't need a shield; they see the rainbow at the end of the tunnel.

Which one is better? The one with the shield because that person knows to never go through it again? Or the one that is out in the open and knows it will receive a few blows but can handle it? Which one is stronger? Now that is the trickiest question of all. Do you shield yourself away from all heartbreak? Or do you let it out, knowing there's a chance for it to be happy?

The way I was raised, I never believed in love. My parents didn't love me and always told me so. How can one love when they aren't shown how? The only thing that helped not destroy everything I knew about love was books. In romance novels, the girl gets her heart broken, but in the end, she ends up with the right guy who treats her like she is the queen. During my teenage years, I always wondered if those kinds of stories were true. Did the princess end up with the prince? The older I got, I realized that love was just a made-up thing. I never experienced it, so how could it be true?

Of course, that all changed the day I met Jason and fell in love. Then I realized that the stories were right; that falling in love was great and almost magical. I had felt like the princess ending up with prince charming. And for that one moment, I believed that my suffering was over and that I would soon see the rainbow. But then, everything changed. I ended up being the girl with the weak heart with a shield around herself. Through the rest of college, I didn't get close to anyone and never let anyone near my damaged heart. Why would I ever think about letting that happen to me again? I wasn't stupid enough to let my heart get healed just for it to break into a million pieces again.

That was when I was only slightly thankful that my parents treated me the way they did. I learned to mask my emotions, to never truly believe someone, and to wear a shield around my broken heart. If the shield were strong, then no one could penetrate it. But then again, fate decided that my heart could be broken once again. That was how I ended up here walking into the office, thinking about that very same quote and the words of my psychology professor.

My heart was broken because of Ashton. I could either do what I did last time, or be the stronger one this time. I could be the one letting my heart slowly heal and looking forward to seeing the rainbow at the end of the tunnel. For once, I wanted to be the one with my heart on my sleeve. I wanted to go outside after the storm and see the beauty of the aftermath, not just the damage. I wanted to see why others put themselves through just so they could feel that little bit of happiness at the end of their suffering.

***

The next day at the office flew by pretty fast, and every time I thought of Ashton, I pushed him aside and focused on other stuff. Today was the day that I decided I wanted to change. I wanted to forget everything that my parents had taught me about love, and start to forge my own. I was going to see the rainbow at the end, whether I wanted to or not. Because maybe, just maybe, I would end up happy.

Most of the day I didn't see Ashton, but I kept busy doing my work. It was only two and I had most of my stuff done. I was more than ready to be home as well. As I was typing an email to one of our clients, my phone buzzed next to me. Reaching for it with one hand, I finished up my sentence with the other. I looked down at it and smiled.

To: Layla
From: Alex
I can tell you're thinking about me right now.

To: Alex
From: Layla
Oh, and how so?

I leaned back in my seat and stared at my phone.

Alex: My Spidey senses are tingling.

Layla: Wow…your senses must be off. I was thinking about another guy.

I hit send and giggled softly to myself. I felt like a teenager staring at my phone waiting for his reply.

Alex: Pfffff right…you're thinking about my

77

foxy ladies from the store, aren't you!

Layla: Oh yeah, I think about the old woman in my spare time.

I couldn't help but feel giddy when he texted me. Something about him brought out my flirtiness, if that was even a word.

Alex: I knew it! :) Anyways, what are you doing?

Layla: Nothing much, just waiting for work to be over.

You could say it was weird that I knew absolutely nothing about Alex, not even his last name. A little voice in the back of my mind couldn't help but chime in every once in a while that, for all we knew, Alex could be a serial killer or be part of a gang. I wouldn't deny that I was slightly worried about that, but for god's sake I was twenty-three years old and I deserved to have some fun for once.

Alex: What time do you get off?

Layla: Around five or so.

I looked around my office and saw I was basically done with everything today, and what wasn't done could be finished tomorrow. I looked at the clock and saw it was about 3:30.

Layla: Actually, I can leave now. Are you busy?

I hadn't even seen Ashton today, so I wasn't worried about leaving early.

Alex: Nope, I'm free. Would it be okay if I came and picked you up to take you to dinner?

Staring down at his reply, I did a mini happy dance in my head. Alex asked me out! Taking a deep breath, I sat there for a few minutes not wanting to reply too quick. I didn't want him to think I was some kind of weirdo glancing at my phone every two seconds, even though I was. After I had let two minutes go by, I replied.

Layla: Sure, that sounds great. :) I'm at 209 Buffalo Drive.

I shut down my computer and started gathering my things. As I smoothed down my pencil skirt, I hoped it would be okay with Alex that I was still in my work clothes. I threw my bag over my shoulder and left my office, heading for the elevators.

"Hey, Judy," I said once I got close.

"Hello. Where are you off to?" she asked, looking up at me.

"I um…I have a date."

"Oh, with who?" Her voice was laced with curiosity.

"This guy named Alex I met at the store yesterday." I grinned, thinking about our first encounter.

"Someone's smitten," Judy said, grinning at me. I blushed and shook my head.

"I am not," I argued but not with much confidence. She just shook her head at me. "It's okay that I leave though, right?" I asked her. I always felt the need to ask Judy's permission more than Ashton's.

"You're fine, Layla, don't worry. Have fun on your date." She smiled at me and I said goodnight to her and left to the elevator. When I got down to the lobby, I looked around for Neena but didn't see her. I was slightly glad cause I didn't want her to question where I was going then have to explain everything. I walked out the doors quickly, just in case Neena decided to pop out somewhere. I swear at times she was like a ninja.

As I waited for Alex, I walked down the street a few doors down and looked through the window of what appeared to be a bookstore. I hadn't known that was there, and I promised myself I would check it out another time. I loved older bookstores like that. Right when you walked in, you're hit with the smell of books, old and new. It was those kinds of places that sold coffee, that somehow had the most comfortable worn-down couches/chairs, and books that I could spend hours reading. Back in college, I would go to the place a few doors down from our apartment and spend hours upon hours there getting lost in studying or reading a book. Just the air of a bookstore was soothing. I knew if I stepped foot in there right now I wouldn't leave until I got kicked out. Smiling through the window, I heard my phone buzz and saw a text from Alex.

Alex: I am outside.

With a sigh, I turned away from the bookstore and headed back to the office building, keeping my eyes open for Alex. When I got closer, I looked to my left and saw Alex leaning against a really nice car in front of Miller Industries. I took in his appearance. He was wearing a gray suit jacket with gray slacks, a white button-up shirt, and a light gray tie. The suit hugged his well-toned body. His blonde hair was smoothed back and over. Staring at him, I felt my knees go little weak. Man, did he look absolutely sexy in a suit!

I walked up to him almost shyly. I felt mediocre in front of him. My brown hair was pulled into a high pony tail, and I had on a tan pencil skirt on with a white blouse, and heels. I didn't put on much makeup on today with only a little eyeliner, eyeshadow, and some lipstick. He was staring up at the building as I came to a stop in front of him.

"Hi," I said nervously, playing with the strap on my bag. He looked down at me and shot me a killer smile. I felt myself relax and smile back at him.

"Wow you look…" he said but trailed off, looking at my work outfit.

"Sorry, it's just my work outfit. I hope that's okay for dinner."

"No, no you look great. Perfect for dinner." He held out his hand for me. "Shall we get going?" he asked in an almost British accent. I laid my hand in his warm big one and nodded.

"We shall," I said replied my best impression of a British accent. Alex chuckled beside me and opened the passenger side of his car for me.

"My lady." He waved his hand in front of the door, and I shook my head at us. Alex seemed to bring out my playful side, and I was already enjoying this date. I buckled myself in while he ran around the front and to the driver's side. I admired the interior of his car and I almost whistled. It was some type of Audi, but I didn't know what model. The soft black leather seemed to wrap my body into itself.

"Nice car," I commented.

"Thank you. This is my favorite." *Favorite? As in, more than one?* I looked at him wide-eyed. "Yes, I have about three cars." *I said that out loud? Stupid mouth.*

I didn't ask how he had three cars, but instead just nodded. He must be pretty loaded to have that many cars. Ashton had three as well.

"Are you hungry now, or do you want to eat in a little bit?" Alex asked, bringing me out of my thoughts.

"I—" I started to say but was interrupted by my stomach, which decided it was time to make mating calls. Blushing, I lowered my head.

"Eat now it is then," Alex said, laughing. My blush got darker. "What would you like to eat?"

"Anywhere's good. I like anything basically, besides seafood," I answered, shrugging and feeling my blush die down.

"I know a great place that isn't too far from here. That okay?"

"That sounds perfect."

We drove in comfortable silence to the

restaurant. It was one of the first times I didn't feel the need to gab the whole ride to avoid silence. Alex pulled up to what looked like a nice restaurant. He got out and before he could open my door for me, I was already out and standing beside the car. He handed his eyes to the valet and grabbed my hand.

"This place has really good food," he said, leading me through the doors and to the front desk. "Table for two," he told the hostess. When she looked at him, her eyes widened, and she quickly grabbed two menus before leading us toward the back. I couldn't help but wonder why she acted the way she did, but I pushed it aside for right now.

"Here you go, Mr. Ryder," the hostess said, handing the menus to us once we were seated. The name Ryder sounded familiar, but I couldn't put my finger on where I had heard it.

"Don't worry about the price," Alex said just as I opened the menu. My eyes almost bulged out of my head. The prices were about as much as it was when I went on my first date with Ashton. Just for a side salad it was $10.99. I stared across at Alex, practically asking him how he could afford these prices. "Choose whatever you want." He sent me a look and I knew to drop it. I looked around for the cheapest thing, but only came up with the side salad. Sighing inaudibly, I knew I couldn't pick something cheap.

"Hello. My name is Nick, and I'll be your server today. What can I get you to drink?" our waiter came up and asked. I opened my mouth to answer with water, but Alex beat me to it.

"Can we get a bottle of your '74 Merlot?"

"Right away, sir." The waiter nodded and walked off. I wasn't a wine expert at all, but I knew enough to know a bottle of '74 Merlot was a lot of money.

"What are you going to get?" he asked me a minute later, setting his menu down.

"I guess whatever pops into my mind when he comes back," I answered, not knowing what to order.

"Can't go wrong with anything here." Right after he closed his mouth, the waiter was back with the bottle of wine. He did that weird thing they do in fancy restaurants in the movies. He poured a little into a glass and waited for Alex to taste it and nod that it was good. I always thought they only did that on movies, but apparently not. I tried not to laugh as Alex smelled the wine and took a small sip. He looked like a weirdo, and I had to choke back a laugh.

"What can I get for you?" the waiter asked a few minutes later after pouring wine into both of our glasses.

"I will have the New York steak with the vegetables," Alex replied. The waiter nodded and turned to me. He didn't even get a notepad out to write it down.

"I, uh, I'll have the BBQ pizza," I said the first thing that came to mind. The waiter raised an eyebrow at me, clearly surprised I ordered pizza instead of a salad or something. He nodded a minute later and left to put our order in.

"Pizza?" Alex asked, amused.

"I'm hungry," I stated and shrugged.

"Here." Alex picked up his wine glass and held it up. I grabbed mine and put it in front of his. "Here's to meeting someone at the grocery store." He grinned then clinked our glasses together. I smiled and took a sip. The wine was good, and I let my body slump back against the booth.

"Your last name is Ryder?" I asked suddenly. I stared across at Alex, feeling that I knew absolutely nothing about him. He nodded and stared at me almost expectantly. "How about we play twenty questions to get to know one another?" I suggested.

"Sure. I'll go first. What is your full name?" He started off easy.

"Layla Kingston," I answered. "I know yours is now Alex Ryder. How old are you?"

"I am twenty-five, almost twenty-six. You?"

"Twenty-three. Where did you go to college and major in?"

"That's two questions, Layla," he chimed but answered anyways. "I went to NYU and majored in business. Now you."

"I also went to NYU and majored in journalism," I answered.

"Wow, we missed each other by only a few years. Your turn."

"Well…I see you're in a suit, so where do you work?" I decided to ask.

"I own my own company, Ryder and Sons," he said. All of a sudden, the name clicked. I froze, staring at Alex.

Alex Ryder! I should have realized that! He was the second most eligible bachelor in New York, a millionaire, and Ashton's enemy and competition.

85

When I was studying up on Ashton's company, I read about Alex but never saw a picture of him. I read that Ashton and he went to the same school and both took over their father's companies around the same time. What was he going to think when he heard I was Ashton's PA?

"I see that you know who I am now," Alex said, trying to break the silence.

"I uh…yeah." I took a sip of my wine. "Sorry, I just didn't expect to be on a date with the second most eligible bachelor in New York," I replied.

"I was starting to wonder when you would figure it out, truthfully," he said, leaning back in the booth while staring at me.

"Sorry, I'm a little slow," I joked.

"Is that going to be a problem?" Alex asked a minute later, looking at me. The way he was staring at me, he looked almost worried about my answer. I was already dealing with one bachelor, and dealing with another wouldn't be a problem. Plus, Alex was different than Ashton; he seemed sweet and sincere.

"No, not at all. It doesn't matter what your status is," I answered truthfully. I had only known him for a day, but I knew Alex wasn't like most stuck up rich people. He shot me a big smile at my answer.

"Okay, good. Back to questions." He rubbed his hands together. "I'll ask you the same. Where do you work?" I hesitated, not really wanting to say where. I mean, if there's bad blood between them, I don't want to get in the way.

"I work at Miller Industries," I finally spat out. He stared at me for a minute before nodding slowly. I sat there waiting for him to ask what I did, but thankfully he didn't.

We asked each other a few more questions before our food came. I learned that Alex had two younger brothers who were about to graduate high school, that his father still helped out at the company, and that his mother was a fashion designer. I told him that I had no siblings, that I lived with my best friend, and used to work at the Sunrise Café before working at Miller Industries.

The rest of dinner we spent asking questions and telling stories. I felt completely comfortable with Alex, and I could feel myself starting to like him. I ignored all of my own protests against continuing with him and let myself have some fun. As I listened to him telling me a story about a prank his brothers pulled on him, I grinned and for the first time since I met Ashton, I forgot about everything and enjoyed my date.

Chapter 7

Ashton

I had been told many times how cold-hearted I was, how cruel and how much of a jackass I could be. Of course, most of that came from women I had slept with. I had gotten used to being called such things, but when Layla said that I was a jackass and didn't care for people's feelings, it hurt more than whenever anyone else said it. The look on her face when I called her a mistake keeps replaying inside my head. I couldn't forget her destroyed expression when she left my apartment.

The moment she walked out my door, I let loose a loud yell and punched the wall. My entire fist went straight through it and pain radiated up my hand and arm. When I pulled it out, my knuckles were split open and bleeding. I stared down at it, not even feeling the pain, only anger toward myself. How could I have said that to her! She was anything but a mistake; in fact, she was the best thing that has happened to me. As the blood started dripping down

88

my hand, I made my way to the bathroom to clean it up and bandage it.

I wish I could take back everything bad I had said to Layla and make it right. But I was too messed up for Layla. She needed someone who could love with everything inside of them, not someone who doesn't believe in love anymore. *It has been four years for god's sake, Ashton. You need to get over her!* I knew the voice right, but I just couldn't get over what she did to me.

"Are you ready for the party tonight?" Nick asked me as we made our way to our cars. It was finally Friday, which meant it was finally my twenty-first birthday and no college for the weekend.

"Hell yes! Glad my parents are letting us use our beach house for the weekend," I answered with a grin.

"I know it's going to be the best party we have ever thrown!" It was going to be. And it was going to be the best night of my life as well.

"Are you going to meet me and Allie there, or do you want to ride with us?" I asked. At the mention of my girlfriend's name, Nick cringed.

"I'll just meet you there."

"Come on, Allie is not as terrible as you think she is!" I was getting tired of how Nick acted every time I mentioned Allie or even when we hung out together. I had been with Allie for two and a half years now, and Nick still didn't like her one bit. As I thought about Allie, I couldn't help but grin.

Allie Montgomery was absolutely perfect. She

had long blonde hair, and a pair of piercing green eyes that could almost see into your soul. She had long tan legs and the perfect body; well, that was a must if she was the cheerleading captain at NYU. Allie was smart, kind, and funny once you got to know her. Even though she was the cheer captain, she was also very smart and could easily make you feel inferior to her in just a matter of moments.

We had met when I had tried out for football and she was trying out for cheer. We bumped into each other coming out of the locker rooms, and the moment I saw her, I fell for her. I didn't see her for a full week until one of our football practices, and she was off to the side with the other cheerleaders. It took me three days to finally get her to say yes to a date with me. For our first date, I took her to a fancy restaurant and then miniature golf afterwards. From that moment on, we became inseparable. Allie was everything I wanted and would ever need.

She got along great with both of my parents, my mother absolutely adored her, and my sister became her best friend. Allie was the perfect student, and girlfriend. Everyone loved her besides Nick; he said there was something off about her, but I never listened. He was just jealous that I had the perfect girlfriend.

Now, two and a half years later and on my birthday, I was going to propose to her. I went with my mom and sister to pick out the best ring I could find. I knew I was only twenty-one and still had a lot ahead of me, but when something feels so right, you have to grab it before it disappears. So tonight, during the party, I was going to take Allie down the shore a ways, where I set up a blanket, candles, and a picnic, and from there I will propose to her.

Nick and I got in our cars and said we'd met up around six to get the beach house ready for the party. It was only one, and Allie had cheer practice until three, so I had some free time to think through my proposal speech for tonight. Driving away from campus, I headed home thinking about everything that needed to be done tonight. When I pulled up in front of our house, I gazed at it. Even though the house was more like a mansion, it felt like home. Most people, when seeing our house, probably thought we weren't a real family and had a lot of problems, but in reality, we were normal. Sure, my father owned his own multimillion-dollar company and my mother was one of the most sought-after lawyers in New York, but we got along great and were raised fairly normal.

We had a nanny when we were younger, but she only watched after us a few times out of the week when neither of my parents could be home. We'd had a few maids, but ever since I was a teenager, my mother said it was mine and my sister's responsibility to clean our rooms, bathrooms, and on our days off, the kitchen and living room. We had a few extra bedrooms for guests, but Mom made us clean them about once every two weeks. Since my mother liked to cook and I didn't mind to either, we never really had a cook. The only time we had someone who cooked were our maids or nanny when our parents were gone.

You would think that with my parents being who

they are, my sister and I would be on our own a lot and we wouldn't be close to them, but it was the exact opposite. They made sure to be home from Friday through Monday with us, and since they were gone sometimes for a few weeks at a time, whenever we saw them we took the opportunity to spend as much time together as we could. I loved my family with everything inside of me, and I was thankful for everything I had in my childhood and teen years.

Unlike a lot of rich spoiled kids, my sister and I were raised to always be nice, friendly, and if we wanted something, we had to work for it. We went to a rich high school where none of the kids had ever had a job in their lives; mommy and daddy paid for everything. During my junior year, I got a job at a local car shop fixing cars during my afternoons when I wasn't playing a sport. Same with my sister; when she was a junior, she got a job at an animal shelter. We were the odd kids out sometimes, but if we never worked for what we wanted, then we wouldn't be where we are now. I was thankful for the way my parents raised me.

I walked inside and called out to see if anyone was home. When I heard a faint "in here" from down the hall, I walked toward my father's study. When I got to the door, I pushed the already halfway opened door and walked inside. My father was leaning over his desk looking over some kind of documents and writing something down. Everyone always said I had my father's drive and personality, and I got my looks from my mother. Seeing my father doing his work, I tried to picture myself doing what he was doing because in just a few years' time, I would at the company with him.

"Hey, Dad," I said, taking a seat across from his desk.

"Ashton, how was class?" my father, John, asked, setting down his pen and looking at me.

"Fine as usual," I replied, shrugging.

"Are you excited for tonight?"

"Yes, definitely." I grinned. I was nervous as hell, but my excitement pushed it down.

"Just don't break anything in the house, don't let things get too wild, and no one in mine and your mother's room," he warned but he smiled. To everyone else, he was a hard business man, but to me, he would always be my funny old man. I knew if I ever needed anything, I could come to him.

"I won't, Dad. I promise."

"Good. Have you figured out what you're going to say to Allie yet when you propose?" When I had told my parents of my plan, they were beyond shocked, but after telling them that this was what I wanted, they were behind me the whole way. They loved Allie almost like their second daughter.

"No, I haven't. What do I say? What did you say to Mom?" I asked, wringing my hands nervously.

"Well, back in those times the men just got on one knee and that's it," he joked.

"Son, I can't tell you what to say. When the moment comes, you will know. Allie is very lucky to have you." I smiled over at my dad and stood up.

"Thank you, Dad. I better get going. Thank you for letting me use the beach house tonight for my party," I said, hugging my dad.

"No problem, son. Have a good night. And, of course, call your mother and let her know tomorrow what happened. Happy birthday, son." With one last nod to my father, I left his office and headed to get everything ready for tonight.

For my party, my parents had our beach house stocked with practically every party food there was and, of course, alcohol. The only condition for letting them supply the alcohol was that no one could drive home after; they even paid for multiple taxis to sit outside to take people home. I was to make sure anyone who drove home was sober or had a designated driver with them. They had also called the local sheriff to let him know there would be a party, in case any noise complaints were called in.

Four hours later

It was now five, and Allie and I were driving to the beach house to get everything done before people started arriving. I practically invited the entire college and told them to be here around six or so. I knew it was early for a party, but if anyone wanted to go play in the water or do stuff on the beach before the sun went down, that was a good time. Plus, some people could get home before the early hours. Nick and I got everything out in the kitchen with bowls of food and all different kinds of alcohol littering the table. Leaving Nick to finish, I went to look for Allie. Not finding her in the living room, I headed to my bedroom.

"Allie?" I called out. I neared my room and

94

thought I heard a noise, so I pushed open my door. Allie stood by my dresser, and she whipped around to see me.

"Ashton," she said, surprised but quickly came over to me and kissed me. She was acting all weird, but I brushed it off. Grabbing her hand, I led her out of my room. As we left my room, I didn't notice my phone was lit up and open.

By seven, the party was in full swing and my parents' beach house was more than packed. It seemed everyone from college really did come. A table was put by the front door that held presents and was starting to overflow. I wasn't expecting people to bring me presents, but hey, I won't reject them. The sun was starting to set, so more and more people were coming in from the beach. As I looked around, I smiled as I saw everyone having a good time. Seeing all the red cups everywhere, I knew it was going to be a bitch to clean up but at the time, I didn't care.

"Hey, Ashton! Happy birthday!" A guy from the football team came up to me.

"Thanks. Hope you're having fun," I said.

"Best party ever, dude!" With that, he was gone. More people started coming inside and dancing in the big living room. I hadn't seen Allie in a while, so I decided I better go and find her. It was a good time to do what I was going to do; not a lot of people were on the beach now, so we would have some privacy. Nick was supposed to be there now lighting the candles for me, so I weaved my way through the crowd trying to find her.

"Hey have you seen, Allie?" I yelled over the

95

music to one of the girls on the cheer squad, I think her name was Bree, but I had no idea.

"No! Haven't seen her!" she slur-yelled at me. I moved on until I reached the other side of the room, and I realized fifteen minutes had passed.

"Have you seen my girlfriend, Allie?" I yelled to some guys on the football team. A few shook their heads but one answered.

"Yeah! I think I saw her head to one of the rooms over there!" He pointed toward the hallway to my room. I had designated that area off limits, but it was okay that Allie was there. Yelling thanks to the guy, I moved past people to the hallway. The room was getting hot with all the sweaty bodies, and I could feel my shirt sticking to my skin.

When I got to the hallway, I patted my front pocket making sure the ring I picked out was still there. I kept finding myself checking my pocket every few minutes. I didn't want to admit it, but I was nervous about Allie's answer. Would she say yes? Or would she say no? The thought of her saying no and not spending the rest of my life with her, made me almost sick. Allie was my everything. To me, it didn't matter that we were only twenty-one; we loved each other, and our parents were happy for us, so what more could we need? In just a year we would graduate and I would work with my dad at his company and Allie would pursue her career as a marine biologist. And maybe a few years after that we would have children and raise them together. I was never really one to think about the future; I had always believed in "live in the here and now" and the rest would follow. But now, with

Allie I could see my future and I wanted it more than anything.

I walked down the hallway, peeking into my sister's room to see if she was there. When I didn't see her, I started to get concerned. As I neared my bedroom, I caught a soft moan coming through the door. That couldn't be? *I wondered as I quickly pushed open on the door. Laying down on the bed, dressed in only her bra and panties, was Allie. She was on top of an unfamiliar guy, who she was kissing and running her hands over.*

"Allie?" I rasped out. She froze and turned her head to stare at me. Her lips were swollen, and glancing at the guy, his were as well, and his hair was messed up from Allie's fingers. The guy's green eyes stared back at me, surprised and confused.

"Ashton." Allie got up off the bed, her tone neutral. I stared at her in hurt. Here I was about to propose to her, and she was cheating on me in my own bed. As I stared at her, I saw no emotion in her green eyes. She almost looked happy in a sick way.

"Allie, what are you doing?" I asked, feeling anger starting to bubble inside of me. I glared at the guy on the bed, who hadn't moved a muscle. "Who the hell are you?"

"My name is Alex. What are you doing bursting in on us?" he asked angrily, standing up.

"Bursting in on you? That is my girlfriend!" I boomed at him and took a step closer to him. "What is she doing in here with you, huh?"

"She came on her own free will. Don't blame me that your girlfriend needs another man to satisfy her." Before he could say anything else, I punched

97

him in the jaw. His head snapped to the side, and I shook my hand, ignoring the pain.

In the next moment, he swung his arm up and hit me in the jaw as well. I tasted blood pooling in my mouth and I saw red. I dove for him and started punching any area I could reach. I barely felt Alex's punches and kept on swinging. I heard yelling and felt a pair of arms pulling me back. I fought against them, but more wrapped around me and I was pulled away from a bleeding Alex.

"Let me go!" I yelled, squirming in whoever's arms. I burst free of them and glared at Alex, not bothering to wipe the blood running from a cut on my eyebrow and one on my lip. "Get the fuck out of my house." I turned and saw a crowd had formed at the door of my room. "The party's over. Get the fuck out of my house!"

I guessed I was pretty frightening because immediately everyone started to scatter. I heard the music come to a stop, and I shouldered past people. A hand landed on my shoulder, but I shook it off, heading to the living room to make sure everyone was leaving. I was not in the mood now for a party. A few stragglers were standing there in surprise, but with one look at me, they moved quickly to the front door.

Sometime during the fight, Allie had run off and I bet she was in a taxi far from here. I was hurt and angry at her. How could she cheat on me? And how could she look at me the way she did, like she was glad I caught her? Whoever that Alex guy is, he is going to pay, *I thought angrily.*

"Ashton." Someone said my name and a hand

landed on my shoulder. I turned and glared at Nick.

"What?" I snapped at him, feeling myself shaking with anger.

"What happened? One second I am walking through the back door and the next, someone is yelling there is a fight," Nick said, looking at me concerned.

"Well, now you can say 'I told you so'. Allie cheated on me." With that, I headed to the kitchen. I grabbed an open bottle of whiskey and took a gulp from it. Instead of cringing from the burning sensation going down my throat, I welcomed it. I took another three gulps before a hand stopped me.

"Ashton, I think that's enough," Nick said, trying to pull the bottle from my grasp.

"No! Go ahead and say I told you so. It would make you feel better, wouldn't it?" I could feel the alcohol coursing its way through my system.

"Ash, I would never say that. She is a bitch to cheat on you."

"Whatever," I muttered and took another gulp. I let the bottle dangle from my grasp by my side. After everything we had been through, Allie had to go and do that, and on my birthday for crying out loud.

I briefly remembered Nick staring at me in concern as I started to drown myself in whiskey.

I woke up the next morning with a killer headache. I peeled my eyes open and looked around with hooded eyes. With weak legs, I stood up off the couch and headed to the bathroom. After I was done in there, I walked to the kitchen for a glass of water. I tried to remember what happened last night, but *my memory was hazy. The banging of plates could be heard in the kitchen, and when I walked in Nick was standing by the stove making some kind of food. Just the smell made me queasy.* Damn, how much did I drink last night? *I wondered. I must have made a sound for Nick turned around.*

"Hey, man, you're up."

"What happened last night, Nick?" I asked, sliding in a chair at the table and holding my head in my hands. My head was pounding and I was confused.

"Umm. You don't remember anything at all?" I shook my head and thought back to the last thing I remembered. I remember greeting people, then trying to find Allie to propose then...My head snapped up. I remembered everything now. I found Allie cheating on me then she disappeared. "There you go," Nick said, once he saw the look on my face.

"Oh god." I moaned and dropped my head into my hands. My phone started ringing then. I looked up and saw Nick reaching for it. "Is it Allie?" I asked, trying to keep the hopefulness out of my voice.

"Sorry, it's your mom." He passed it to me and I answered.

"Hello?"

"Ashton? What happened?" my mother yelled through the phone. I pulled it away from my ear. How did she know what happened already?

"W-What do you mean?" I decided to ask just in case it was something different.

"Five million dollars has been stolen out of your

account!" I stood up quickly.

"What? How?" I asked.

"We got a call from the bank and they notified us. You transferred five million dollars into Allie's account?" my mom shrieked.

"N-no, I—" I froze, remembering when I had walked in on Allie in my room before the party. She looked suspicious and was acting weird all throughout the party. My eyes widened as I remembered seeing my phone lit up and open on my dresser when I didn't do it. Ashton, you're a fucking idiot! You forgot to erase your account number from your phone! *The voice in my head yelled at me.*

I couldn't help but suddenly start crying. "M-Mom, Allie stole my money and ran off."

Everything changed the day Allie stole from me and ran off. I turned into a different person; I was a shell of what I used to be. I wasn't that carefree, loving, outgoing guy anymore. There was nothing inside. The rest of college, I slept with anything that walked and didn't care who I hurt. If I was going to hurt, then everyone else was too. I never heard from Allie again after that. I tried to reach her parents, but they never answered, I even went to see them, but the house was abandoned.

Allie had used me to get money and when she did, she disappeared. For a whole year, I went through stages of being pissed to almost depressed. The only way I knew to get rid of my emotions was to have sex with women. I barely graduated college, and partied way too much. My family didn't know what to do with me, and my father forced me to work with him at the company.

After the first year, I started to realize what I was doing and stopped, well, with the partying anyways. I decided then and there that I would never let another woman get into my heart. I was not going to be broken and used again.

Once I had gotten my act together, my father decided to step down and let me take over. I was honestly glad that I now had something that got my mind off of everything. I slowly forgot about Allie, the good times we had, and only once in a while thought about her. But now, being with Layla, I was starting to become the way I used to be. I found myself smiling while thinking of her, and I could picture being with her. Could I let go of my past and finally be happy again? Or was I going to let what Allie did haunt me for the rest of my life?

Chapter 8

Layla

The rest of my date with Alex was great. We talked about everything, and I couldn't stop laughing at his stories. The night had gone by fast and before I knew it, Alex was walking me to my door. I loved his company and I felt like a totally different person when I was with him, but of course, I couldn't stop comparing him to Ashton. From the way he talked, his gestures, to even how his body looked compared to Ashton's. Ashton had this hold on my brain and it was starting to piss me off. I couldn't go one second without thinking of his blue eyes or that smirk.

I had forced all of the thoughts about him to the back of my mind the whole night, but the moment Alex left they came rushing back like a tidal wave. As I lay in bed staring up at the ceiling, I couldn't help but wonder if Ashton was thinking about me too, or about Natasha. Even just thinking her name made me bitter. She was everything I wasn't. I knew Ashton should be with her, since they would make a great couple, but just thinking of them together made my blood boil. Yes, I was going insane. After everything that Ashton had put me through, I still liked him. It was pathetic, but I couldn't stop. I was the addict and he was the drug.

Ungrateful. That was one word that kept flashing through my mind ever since Alex left. Here I was with a sweet, caring, hot guy who would be perfect for me, and who I already agreed to go on another date with. And just a few hours after I went on a dinner date, I am thinking of another guy. A guy who doesn't want anything to do with me, who hurts me at almost every corner, who is my boss, and who is probably not good for me. But I have seen the side that no one else has—a loving, caring, and broken guy. I liked who I was with Alex, even though it kind of felt like he was treating me like I was fragile. But I also liked how I felt with Ashton; he made my skin tingle and my heart beat fast. Sure, we argued, but I liked that.

Wow, Layla. You have just dug a hole for yourself.

I spent the whole night tossing and turning thinking about both guys. I went to work feeling just as confused as I did last night. Work was uneventful and boring. I hadn't seen Ashton at all, and I was glad. I didn't know what I was feeling at the moment, and I knew seeing him would make it just as hard. I was distracted all day, and I couldn't have been happier when five o'clock hit and I could go home. As I took a taxi home, I made the dangerous decision to bring Kacey into this. I needed her opinion, and I was tired of dealing with it on my own. She didn't know about Alex, and I wasn't looking forward to her reaction to such news being kept from her.

Fortunately, when I got home, Kacey wasn't there yet so I had time to go over what I was going to say. It was sad that I was more scared of my friend than I was with basically anything else. I changed my clothes and was staring at the tv mindlessly, waiting for Kacey. About an hour after I got home, I heard the keys in the door and started bracing myself for my upcoming speech.

"Oh, good, you're home. I have had the longest day of my life, I swear," Kacey said upon seeing me on the couch and setting her things down. With her stuff thrown carelessly on the ground by the door, she jumped on the couch. I honestly didn't know much about Kay's job, but I knew she was under the director at *Vogue*. She did something with helping make clothes. Man, I really was a terrible best friend, I knew nothing about my best friend's job, or even what was going on with her life. I'd been so caught up in mine that I hadn't been around for Kacey.

"What happened?" I asked. From now on I needed to be a better friend to her.

"My boss didn't like any of the designs me and the other designers made, so we have to redo all of it. All thirty-something designs for the winter line need to be re-designed in two weeks for the next issue," Kacey said.

"Man, that's…intense."

"Tell me about it. I want to say sorry beforehand

because I may not be home much in the next few weeks, or if I become grouchy," she said, looking over at me.

"That's okay." There was a moment of silence, and I knew this was the time to talk to her. Taking a deep breath, I opened my mouth but instead a knocking sounded on the door before it flew open. In came Neena, slamming the door behind her and flopping on the other side of me on the couch.

"I hate guys!" She grunted and laid her head back. Both me and Kacey looked at each other before turning to her. I wasn't as surprised as I first was when Neena barged into our place. She had been over here so many times in the last three weeks that neither Kacey or I were surprised by her visits.

"Why?" Kacey asked, leaning around me to see Neena.

"Liam is just so stupid! Ever since the night at the gala, we have been getting closer, but he hasn't asked me out yet. It has been almost a week! I've given him plenty of hints."

"Well maybe he just wants to take it slow," I suggested.

"But I don't want him to." She practically whined.

"Just give him some time, Neena. He will ask you out. If he doesn't, then he is an idiot. Layla and I will go over there if he doesn't," Kacey said, grinning at Neena.

"Thanks, guys."

"No problem," I said than chewed on my bottom lip. "I need your help now," I finally blurted out.

Now was as good time as ever. They both turned to me, waiting. "I…"

"You're pregnant!" Kacey suddenly shouted.

"No!" I shouted, my eyes wide. "Where the hell did you get that?"

"You just seem very nervous, and well, that was the first thing that popped in my head," she confessed, shrugging.

"Okay, well, I have two guys who I really like, but I don't know what to do." I told both of them about how I met Alex and dinner last night. Then I told them everything with Ashton. They both were silent, thinking over everything I told them.

"Wow. Who knew you would have two of the world's most eligible bachelors begging for your attention?" Kacey joked.

"Only Alex is, though. Ashton couldn't care less," I added, playing with my fingers in my lap. "I don't know what to do."

"How hot is Alex Ryder?" Neena asked.

"Very. He's got these gorgeous deep green eyes, a killer smile, and not to mention a nice body." I sighed, thinking about him. "Plus, he is super sweet, funny, and caring, even for a millionaire. He doesn't act like he has money."

"Now what about Ashton?"

"He's just as hot as Alex. With his bright blue eyes, soft brown hair, and when he sends me one of his rare smiles it makes him beyond gorgeous. He also has a nice body. Sometimes he doesn't show it, but he can be sweet, caring, and protective."

"I think I know what you have to do," Neena said.

107

"What?"

"You need to go on a real date with Alex. Afterwards, see what you feel and if you don't feel butterflies or anything close to what you feel when you're with Ashton, then you know what you have to do." She sent me a small smile and put her hand on my shoulder.

"I agree with her," Kacey added.

"Thank you, guys." I reached and put my arms around their shoulders. We sat in silence staring at the tv.

"What are we doing for dinner?" Kay asked, breaking the peaceful silence. Neena and I laughed but got up. We ended up ordering Chinese again and spent the night having fun.

***

The week flew by and it was finally Friday. I only briefly saw Ashton, but he mostly stayed clear of me. When he had lunch meetings or anything, I just texted reminding him instead of going to his office. We were both avoiding each other and I couldn't help but feel sad. I missed seeing him, even if it was when we were arguing. I felt like I was missing something inside of me every time I passed his office and didn't see him.

I was more than ready to go on a date with Alex so I could sort my feelings out. Yesterday, he called me asked me out for tonight and I quickly agreed. I needed to get my feelings sorted. I never thought something like this would happen to me, and now that it was I didn't know what to do.

Closing down my computer, I gathered my stuff and left my office. It was a five past five o'clock, and Alex said he'd pick me up at my apartment at five-thirty. That gave me twenty-five minutes to get home and change into something more comfortable. I had no idea what Alex had planned, so once I got home I would text him.

Saying a quick goodbye to Judy and with one last glance at Ashton's office, I left the building and headed toward home. Even though today was boring, I got paid and that helped brighten my mood. I was second-guessing looking for another job. This one paid a lot, more than what I had made in a year at the café. This paycheck was almost $4,000. Even if Ashton drove me nuts, I actually didn't mind my job. I mean, who wouldn't mind getting paid that much every two weeks? I may have almost peed my pants when I saw the number.

I got home in five minutes, so I quickly paid the taxi guy and booked it upstairs to get dressed. As Kacey had said on Monday, she wasn't home like the rest of the week. The place had been quiet, and I didn't realize how boring it was without someone here. Walking through the front door, I sent Alex a quick text asking what to wear as I stripped out of my work clothes. When my phone buzzed, I ran to it but ended up getting my legs twisted in a pile of clothes and fell on the floor. Groaning, I reached up and felt around for my cellphone. Feeling it, I grabbed it and read Alex's reply.

To: Layla
From: Alex

Something warm.

Yeah, that helps a lot, I thought sarcastically. Placing my phone back on my bed, I untangled my legs and stood up. Going to closet, I scanned the contents wondering what would be good. Looking at the clock, I saw I only had fifteen minutes until he got here. I pulled on a pair of black skinny jeans, and a cute, thick red and blue plaid long-sleeved shirt. Since my hair was in waves today, it was starting to frizz, so I grabbed a gray beanie and pulled it on my head. Reaching into my closet, I pulled out my favorite pair of brown boots. Looking in the mirror, I saw I looked pretty good considering I had been at work all day. Putting on a new layer of lipstick, I grabbed my cellphone and bag before leaving the apartment.

Just as I left through the front doors, Alex's Audi pulled up to the curb. Before he could get out, I opened the passenger door and slid in. He had the heater going and I was glad he did. The sun was about to go down, and it was starting to get chilly.

"Hey," I breathed.

"Hi. You look great," he said, shooting me a smile.

"Thank you. You don't look too bad yourself," I added once I saw his outfit. He was in a pair of dark blue jeans, and a gray long-sleeved shirt. His blonde hair was brushed up into a coif. He looked so sexy in casual attire.

"So, do you want to eat first or do the activity I had planned?" he asked, pulling away from the curb slowly.

"Hmmm. What's the activity?"

"Can't say, it's a surprise." He shot me a big grin, clearly excited about whatever we were doing.

"Let's do the activity first," I suggested. I wasn't that hungry right now anyways. I grabbed a late lunch today, so I would be good for another few hours.

As Alex drove through traffic, I looked out the window listening to the radio playing softly in the background. I was curious as to where he was taking us. All different kinds of things ran through my mind, and I bit back questioning him where we were going. About twenty minutes later, he pulled in front of the Rockefeller Center. I turned to him, confused and excited. He shot me a grin and slid out of the car. Swiftly, he came to my side and let me out. I moved to the sidewalk and stared around like a tourist. I was so busy gawking at all the tall buildings around us that I didn't hear Alex talking to the valet or when the car left. A hand on my lower back brought be back to reality, and I looked up at an amused Alex.

"Ready to go? Or want to gawk some more?" he asked teasingly. I stuck my tongue out at him childishly, and let him lead me under this archway and down appeared to be a walkway.

"Where are you taking me?" I couldn't help but question.

"You'll see." I frowned at him but glanced around at the pretty trees as we walked. Not even three minutes later, Alex came to a stop in front of me, almost making me crash into him. "Okay, close your eyes."

"No, what if you're trying to kill me!" This wouldn't be the best place to do it, but I could see plenty of places to hide a body.

"Layla, I'm not going to kill you. Just please close your eyes." With a look from Alex, I sighed and closed my eyes. "Okay, how many fingers am I holding up?"

"Eight?" I questioned. I must have guessed wrong because I felt his hand wrap around my cold one, and he started pulling me forward. As we walked a few feet, I could feel the air getting colder. I tucked my free hand in my back pocket, wanting to stay warm. A minute later I felt Alex's warm breath on my cheek making me shiver.

"Open," he said softly. I opened my eyes and gasped. In front of me was an ice skating rink, but not just any ice skating rink; it was the Rockefeller one. *I should have known that.* I had always wanted to come here but never have. I turned to Alex with a wide grin.

"We are ice skating?" I almost shrieked.

"That's okay, right?" he questioned, looking nervous for a second. I took a step toward him and gave him a big hug.

"It's perfect. I've always wanted to come here." I pulled away, looking at the rink like a child does at Disneyland. There were only a few people on the ice, making me even happier. I didn't know how to skate, and I didn't want to fall in front of a bunch of people. I grabbed Alex's hand and tugged him toward the booth to get skates. I heard him chuckle behind me but kept pulling him until we came to a stop at the booth.

"Hello. Two for ice skating?" the older man asked.

"Yes please," I answered.

"Okay that will be fifty-five dollars," he said. I almost winced at the price but before I could even say anything, Alex was handing the money over to the man.

"Keep the change," he said.

"Thank you. What size shoe?"

"Seven," I answered, and Alex answered, "Eleven."

The man handed me a pair of white seven skates and Alex a black pair. Feeling giddy, I made my way to a bench to put my skates on. I was nervous but my excitement masked it. We were quiet as we sat side by side lacing up our skates. Alex stood up and held his hand out for me. I placed mine in his and stood up shakily. It was weird having to balance on a thin blade, and if you turned your foot wrong you would sprain your ankle. With the help of Alex's hand keeping me steady, we made it to the entrance of the ice. I let go of his hand as he stepped onto the ice. I stood back, feeling slightly more nervous. I didn't want to fall and make a fool out of myself in front of Alex.

"Are you ready?" I nodded at Alex, but kept my gaze on the smooth white ice. How was I supposed to skate on that with just a thin blade? "Have you never ice skated before?" he asked, standing in front of me. We were blocking the entrance, but I didn't care.

"N-no, I haven't," I admitted, stuttering a little.

"It's okay. It isn't too hard. Just hold onto me

113

and I'll teach you." With a reassuring smile, I nodded and gripped his hands. I lifted my legs and stepped onto the ice. My legs were wobbly, but I kept my legs straight and still as Alex slowly pulled me further onto the ice. My grip was hard around his hands, but he didn't object. He skated backwards with a grace that made me jealous.

"See not too hard." He kept leading me around for a few minutes while my feet and legs adjusted. "Think you're okay to let go of me?" I nodded, feeling more comfortable. Slowly, like a dad does when letting go of a child's bike when they're learning to ride it, Alex withdrew his hands until I was left moving at a snail pace. He skated a little ahead of me, and I moved my legs trying to reach him. When I didn't fall, I beamed over at him.

"Did you see that? I didn't fall!" I exclaimed louder than I should have but I didn't care. Feeling more confident now, I bent my legs slightly and moved my feet a tad bit fast than a snail pace. For some reason, as I skated slowly next to Alex, I thought of the movie *Ice Princess*. I could almost imagine myself being an ice skater and moving effortlessly across the ice. I was too distracted daydreaming so I didn't watch my feet, and I ended up tripping over them and landed on the ice. My butt hit the cold ice and I made an "oomph" sound. *Nice, Layla, nice.*

Ahead of me, I saw Alex grinning and holding back a laugh. I didn't know why, but I suddenly started to laugh. I sat on the cold ice laughing at myself until Alex reached me.

"You okay?" he asked, chuckling softly.

"Yeah, I'm good." I giggled. Alex extended a hand out for me and I grabbed it, pulling myself up. He must not have seen me picking myself up because he pulled me up and I ended up smashed against his chest. Since he had done this before, he positioned perfectly where we would fall. I grinned up at him in thanks. I only vaguely noticed someone with a camera snapping pictures of us from afar.

I spent the next hour or so getting better, and soon I was skating pretty fast and even learned to do a small spin. I had only fallen three times, and I was proud of myself. Alex clearly had experience, but he skated alongside me telling me ways to put my feet and to hold out my arms for more balance. The sun had set a long time ago, and the moon appeared low in the sky. The lights that surrounded the rink were on and made the ice sparkle. Something about it felt magical.

I finally had to get off the ice when I noticed my fingers were turning blue and I couldn't feel my face. I skated to the entrance and onto the carpet, where I almost fell. The carpet was a lot different than the ice, and it took me a minute to get adjusted. I wobbled over to the bench where our shoes were, and sat down. I didn't realize how Jell-O-y my legs felt until I sat down. My legs felt stiff and I knew I would be really sore tomorrow.

After Alex and I got our skates off, we walked hand and hand back to the booth to return our skates.

"Did you have fun?" he asked as we walked back to the front to get the car.

"I had a blast. Thank you so much."

"Good, I'm glad you had fun. Now let's eat. I'm starving." The moment I got in the car, I put my hands in front of the vents that were blowing hot air. The car was starting to warm up when Alex peeled away from the curb, and I felt my cold bones thawing.

Alex took me to a cute little Italian place that had amazing food. We spent almost two hours there just talking and laughing with each other. Just being around Alex was comfortable, relaxing, and great. The night had flown by and before I knew it, it was ten o'clock at night and he was pulling up to my building. I met Alex around the car, and he grabbed my hand. The walk up to my place, he was silent and rubbing his thumb across my knuckles, making goosebumps appear up and down my arms. I came to a stop outside my door and faced him.

"I had a great night. Thank you for everything," I said sincerely up at him.

Everything about this night was perfect.

"You're welcome. I had a great time as well. You're amazing, Layla." I watched as he leaned his head down, and my eyes closed on their own. His soft lips met mine and his hand reached up to cup my cheek. Our lips moved in sync, and I could taste a little bit of wine from his lips. My knees weakened, and my hands gripped his forearm holding me up. We finally parted, catching our breath. He leaned his forehead against mine, and I stared up into his green eyes.

"Have a good night. Don't dream too hard about me." He smiled at me. He pecked my lips one last time before pulling away. I watched as he walked away until I couldn't see him anymore. I opened my door and leaned against it once it was shut.

With shaky legs, I walked to my room. Not feeling like taking a shower at the moment, I changed into my PJs, washed my face, and sat on my bed. I sat there thinking about tonight and about our kiss. I reached up and felt my semi-swollen lips; they didn't tingle the way it did when I kissed Ashton. Flopping down on my back on my bed, I thought over everything. From Ashton to Alex, to how our both of our dates compared, then to my feelings about each person. I stared at the ceiling feeling a sudden calm feeling surround me. I had made my decision on who I wanted.

Chapter 9

Ashton

All week I was AWOL. I was either holed up in my office or here at home. I didn't want to see Layla because my feelings were a mess at the moment. I didn't know how I feel toward her, or if I was ready to move on from what Allie did to me. I avoided her at all costs this whole week and now that it was Friday, I was actually starting to regret it. Even though I didn't really see her much at work, I missed those few times I did. I knew I was acting pathetic avoiding Layla like I was still in high school, but I knew just one look from her and I would be on my knees acting for forgiveness quicker than someone could say ice cream.

Being with Layla made me feel things I hadn't felt in quite a long time, not since Allie. She made me feel like my old self, and I wouldn't deny that I missed being him. I missed being carefree, laughing with my friends, loving someone. But at the same time, those feelings scared me and brought

118

unwanted questions to mind. Was she going to do the same thing as Allie? Was I going to be left a shell like last time? I wish I could stop those thoughts, but I couldn't. Allie broke me beyond repair. I didn't know if I could ever get back to the way I was before.

Before Layla, I was fine being the way I was. I was fine working almost every day, being cold and heartless toward everyone, fine using a girl and not caring about how she reacted. I was fine being a shell. But with those few loving moments with her, I didn't want to go back to my old ways. I wanted to change for the better. Those few moments made me realize that what I was doing wasn't healthy or right. I liked how Layla was different than the other girls I'd been with, I loved how she argued with me and made my blood boil. I loved how just one look and I could practically see everything she was feeling and thinking.

I sat behind my desk thinking about everything. I wanted to change, and I wanted Layla to change me. With that thought in mind, I stood up and walked out of my office toward her. Now was as good time as any to finally let her know how I felt. I was just hoping that she would forgive me for everything I had done and said to her. Taking a deep breath, I opened her door and stepped in. I was expecting to see her at her desk working, but instead I was surrounded with darkness and an empty chair. Layla wasn't here. Frowning, I turned and headed over to Judy.

"Judy, do you know where Layla is?" I asked, coming to a stop in front of her. I really needed to talk to her, and I didn't want to wait another minute.

"She left about twenty minutes ago."

"Where?"

"I don't know. I think she had plans," Judy said, looking at me almost apologetically.

"Oh." I tried to leave out my saddened tone but failed.

"Just call her tomorrow, sweetie. I know she isn't doing anything because she told me she would just be sitting around at home," Judy said. *Tomorrow? I can't wait until tomorrow!* Judy must have seen the look on my face because she put her hand on my shoulder. "Ashton, she is probably busy, and it's a Friday. Let her be until tomorrow."

I sighed and lowered my head. She was right, but tomorrow, first thing in the morning, I would be at Layla's house. Telling Judy thanks, I went back to my office to finish up a few things. That, of course, turned out impossible since Layla was on my mind the entire time. I didn't know how many times I reached for my phone to call Layla, but every time I stopped myself from going through with it. Judy was right; she was probably busy. If I wanted her to forgive me, then I had to give her space for the moment.

The night went by agonizingly slowly. I stayed at the office until seven or so, then headed home to try and get some rest. I also wanted to go over what I was going to say to Layla and how to get her to forgive me for my stupidity over the past month and a half.

Month and a half? Have I really known Layla that long? That time period wasn't all that long, but to have already fallen for her? It was a short amount of time. It took me longer than that to fall for Allie. It was weird feeling like this only after a month, but I didn't want to waste any more time.

The whole night I tossed and turned, trying to get my mind onto something else. When the sun started to peek into my room, I had only gotten maybe two hours of sleep, if that. Even though I hadn't slept, I felt more energized than I had in a while. I knew it was because I was going to finally tell Layla what I felt about her, and I was going to tell her everything about Allie. I was hoping my heartbreak story would help her in forgiving me easier. I got up and headed to the bathroom before noticing the clock. It was only a little after six in the morning, and there was no way Layla was up at this time on a Saturday. I almost groaned out loud knowing I had to wait a few more hours before heading to her place. After going to the bathroom and splashing cold water on my face, I threw on a pair of PJ bottoms before heading downstairs. I might as well get something to eat and read the paper before getting ready. I had time to kill.

My newspaper came earlier than most, and I knew it was already outside. I unlocked my door and reached out, grabbing my rolled-up paper. I headed back to the kitchen to make a cup of coffee and set the paper on the counter. A giddy feeling was welling inside of me, and I knew it was because I was going to see Layla. I didn't mind the feeling because for once I was feeling something other than anger, emptiness, or nothing. I sat down on a stool and unrolled the paper. What I saw next made my body freeze and my eyes widen.

Millionaire bachelor has a girlfriend!

On the front of the *New York Times* was a picture of Layla smiling up at Alex Ryder. The guy who cheated on with my ex, the guy I hated with everything I had, and my business enemy. I stared at the front page, looking at Layla grinning up at Alex. She was grinning so widely, and I couldn't remember if I had ever seen her look like that before. My giddy feeling disappeared and left nothing inside of my chest. I read the small article below the picture.

It seems our very own bachelor Alex Ryder has gotten himself a girl. A girlfriend? Or just a new plaything? From the looks of the picture above, they look pretty cozy with each other, and were seen together ice skating at Rockefeller Center. Grins and laughs were present all night before they left hand in hand. We don't know who the lucky girl is, but if she has captured the attention of Ryder, then she must be special, and we have to say they look great together. An insider said Alex looked practically smitten over the mystery girl. What's going to happen with these love birds? Do we hear wedding bells soon?

As I read the article, my stomach dropped lower and lower. What was she doing with Alex of all people? And what was she doing ice skating with him? *Because she has moved on, idiot.* I wanted to deny that, but the longer I stared at the picture, I felt my heart somehow breaking, or what was left of it. I should have known this would happen. I should have known she would choose someone else. I could feel my wall starting to come back down around me and my heart hardening. I shouldn't have even thought this time would be different; whenever something good comes my way it finds a way to turn out disastrous or wrong.

If Layla had moved on, then I should as well. The best way not to get your heart broken is to pretend you don't have one. Tearing my eyes away from the paper, I threw it across the room and ran my fingers through my hair. With my walls down and forcing myself to forget about Layla all together, I headed up to my room and grabbed my cellphone. I knew I probably shouldn't be doing this, but I clicked the number and pressed call. If Layla was going to be with another guy, then I would be with another girl. I was going to do what I do best.

"Hello?" The female voice came through the phone.

"Come over to my place," I answered then hung up. I paced my room, resisting the urge to punch something. My knuckles had barely recovered from the last time I hit my wall. I listened to the sudden pitter-patter of rain hitting my window. I looked outside, watching dark clouds coming toward town and bringing with it rain. When a knock sounded downstairs, I stalked downstairs clenching my jaw and throwing open the door. Standing there in a skin-tight dress was Natasha. Growling low, I grabbed her waist and pulled her inside and up against the wall. Before anything could escape her lips, I slammed mine down on hers and kissed her with all of the anger inside of me.

***

Layla

I woke up this morning to the sound of rain hitting my window. I rolled over snuggling deeper in my covers, not wanting to get up. Knowing it was Saturday didn't help either. The sound of the rain was soothing, and I loved it. As I listened to the rain, I suddenly remembered last night. I quickly sat up and looked around. I had forgotten all about last night! Looking over at my clock, I saw it was nine in the morning. *Shit! I have something I have to do!* I quickly scrambled out of my bed, only to get my body tangled with my covers and fall to the ground. I groaned, trying to ignore the stabbing pain going up my elbow and knee. Knowing I would probably have a bruise tomorrow, I untangled my legs and booked it to the bathroom.

Quickly showering, I let my hair hang down my shoulders air drying as I threw on a pair of blue skinny jeans and a cute long sleeve gray shirt. I wanted to look cute, but not like I was trying to either. Putting on a little foundation to hide my bags, as well as some mascara and lip gloss, I slipped on a pair of gray flats before grabbing my bag and heading out. I wanted to do this sooner because it would give me time to say what I want to say. Thankfully our building had a cover, so I wasn't getting wet as I hailed a cab. I quickly ran out and slid inside the taxi, rattling off Ashton's address.

Yes, I chose Ashton. I knew it wasn't the greatest choice considering everything he had said and done, but being with Alex was nothing like being with Ashton. Yes, I had a great time with Alex and we got along great, but there wasn't that spark that I had with Ashton. There wasn't that passion burning inside of me waiting to burst free, and my skin didn't tingle the way it did when Ashton briefly touched me. Ashton and I had a lot to work out, and I wasn't going to let him off the hook for what he has done to me. I was going to make him grovel for a little bit and maybe even beg before I forgive him.

Deep down I knew Ashton had been hurt before, and that was why he acted the way he did. Having been hurt before, I could see he had built a shield around himself; becoming closed off and rude is his way of protecting himself. Being hurt didn't excuse what he had done, but at least there's a reason for doing so instead of him just doing it out of satisfaction.

I liked him more than I should, but I knew it would be a little while before I could come to love him. I didn't even know if I was capable of love anymore, but liking was better than nothing. I wondered what I'd do if he didn't feel the same way back. It was okay if he didn't. I just had to tell him and get it out. As long as he knows and doesn't like me back, then I can start to move on instead of wondering if he feels the same. It's better to have known than to have lost. I didn't want to not say anything and years later wonder what would have happened. No more what-ifs. For once, I was going to be rash and careless with my feelings.

I hadn't told Alex yet, but I would after. I just wanted to talk to Ashton first before saying anything. Even if he didn't feel the same about me, I would still tell Alex. I would not be that person who strings him along when I didn't feel the same about him. I just hope he wouldn't get too made, and that we could be friends. I would rather be friends with him than nothing, and I hope he would as well. Alex was a great guy and deserved someone who could love him with everything they have, not with just a small piece of their heart. I didn't want to hurt him, and that's why I had decided to do this early, so I could tell him before he starts to feel something for me. I wanted to stop anything before it was too late.

The taxi came to a stop and I sat frozen on the seat, staring up at the building. Was I ready to go up there? I was slowly getting out of the taxi, but apparently it wasn't fast enough for the driver because he practically yelled at me to get out. As the taxi drove away, I stood there in the rain staring up at the building. Now that I was here, I was starting to get nervous. I could feel the rain starting to soak my clothes and hair, a few drops rolling down my face. I knew I looked like a weirdo standing out in the rain, so after a few minutes I headed inside, almost completely soaked.

I wondered what the people here thought of me as I walked to the elevator. I'd been here plenty of times in my work clothes, but I've also come out looking like crap and crying. The workers probably thought I was a whore or something. Rain had pooled inside my shoes and I could feel my toes tingling from the slight cold. Water was starting to drip off the ends of my hair, and I was sure there was a puddle underneath me. I played with my fingers as I rode to Ashton's floor, going over everything I wanted to say. Last night as I lay in bed, I came up with a whole speech and I worded it perfectly for today.

Finally, the elevator dinged opened and I walked out biting my bottom lip heading to his door. With a deep breath and a shaky hand, I reached up and knocked on his door.

"Layla, you can do this," I chanted under my breath to myself as I waited for him to answer. "Just remember what you said this morning. Don't let him off so easy." Nodding to myself like a psychopath, I rubbed my sweaty palms on my wet jeans.

The door finally opened, and my heart sank faster than the Titanic. Standing in front of me in nothing but one of Ashton's work shirts was Natasha. The shirt barely went to the top of her thighs, and the front buttons only had four of the seven done up, leaving a sizable amount of cleavage on display. I took in her appearance and noticed her blonde hair was everywhere like someone's hands have been in it, her lips were swollen, and on her neck looked to be a hickey.

127

"I, uh—" I stuttered out, not having even thought about if Ashton had someone here.

"You're Ashton's assistant, right?" Natasha asked in a soft accent. I couldn't pin point what kind it was, but I wasn't surprised she wasn't from America. All I could do was nod dumbly.

"Babe, who's there?" I heard Ashton call out from somewhere inside. If my heart could have dropped any lower, it did. I stood in front of the beautiful, almost naked model, looking like a drowned rat from the rain. My hair stuck to my neck and forehead, and I bet my clothes were hanging off of me soaked in water.

Standing there looking at the woman dressed in Ashton's shirt, I felt broken. Of course, Ashton would be with Natasha. He wouldn't be thinking about stupid little me. Hearing him call her babe, I knew he had to be somewhat serious with her. I was so stupid thinking I could just show up here assuming he would be alone and wanting to be with me. I completely forgot about Natasha and him being an item. Feeling whatever was left of my heart shattering, I forced a thin smile.

"Sorry for interrupting something. I better go. Please tell Ashton it wasn't me," I said softly, almost in a whisper. Natasha looked at me funny but nodded at my request. I sent her a shaky smile before turning down the hall. I neared the hallway where it turned and stood hidden by it, looking at the door. I watched as the door started to close when Ashton came up and kissed Natasha roughly on the lips, his hands wrapping around her skinny waist. I watched with a broken heart as the door closed on them kissing. Feeling tears pool in my eyes, I dragged my feet to the elevator and then to the front doors.

He didn't feel the same. He never would. I stepped outside and into the rain, realizing I couldn't have Ashton. He was taken and looked to be fine being taken by Natasha. I was so stupid thinking I could actually show up, confess my feelings and be with Ashton. I hadn't even thought about any other scenarios, like him being with someone else. I didn't know how much I actually liked him until I saw him kissing her, feeling my heart shatter. The rain mixed with my tears rolling down my face.

Tears blurred my vision as I walked in the direction of home in the rain. It felt like the clouds were crying with me feeling my pain. As I walked home, I didn't feel sad or hurt. I felt nothing. Numb. Knowing that he now was taken, I knew I had to do what was right, despite my feelings. I now knew what it felt like to let go of someone I really loved for them to be happy.

I walked home in the pouring rain quietly crying, wrapping my arms around my middle as if to hold me together because if I didn't, I would fall apart.

Chapter 10

Layla

The rest of Saturday and Sunday passed in kind of a blur. I was inside my own bubble, not really seeing or hearing anything. When I had gotten home from Ashton's, my entire outfit and body were soaking wet, so the first thing I did was hop in the shower. Actually, all I did in there was let the water run over me as I stared at the wall. I was still trying to wrap my mind around everything that had happened. When Sunday rolled around, I was still as confused as I was the day before, but slightly more coherent.

Every time anything happened that involved Ashton, I seemed to get clobbered, and I was tired of it. He pushed me away, and I somehow came right back. He was sweet to me, and I fell even more. Now, when I'm ready to confess my feelings to him, he's with someone else. I was fed up. When I was younger, I was so desperate to feel loved that I welcomed the notion of getting my heart broken because if it was broken, than that meant I had something real and good. But now I realized how stupid I was, and I was tired of getting my heart broken. What I really needed right now was to be by myself. I needed to figure out what I wanted, and in order to do that, I needed time alone.

It seemed like right when my life was at an okay point—I was fine with my job, my life, and my friends—something had to go and ruin it. I hadn't known it, but the moment I ran into Ashton at that bar my life had done a 180. My heart fell for someone again when I didn't think I could. I quit my awful job and was now working at a multimillion-dollar company making good pay. I'd met new people that I'm coming to love as my best friends, and most of all, I'd come to realize what I need in my life.

I was finally coming out of the shell I had built all around me when I was with my parents. I was putting myself at risk and finally being carefree. I was tired of my parents holding me back, and me feeling like I was still with them. It had been four and a half years, and I hadn't heard from them not even once. I could be dead for all they knew, and they didn't care. I'd always felt their presence lurking over me all my life. I was not that little innocent thirteen-year-old who let her parents beat her anymore. I am twenty-three, almost twenty-four, with a new life. I was not skittish anymore, and I was not afraid. It was time for me to live my life the way I wanted to; no more letting people do it for me, or listening to my parents' voices in the back of my mind.

That didn't mean I was going to party every night, hook up with random guys, or even quit my job. I was just going to be alone for a while, hang out with my friends, and get my priorities straight. I had just committed to my plan when Kacey and Neena suddenly burst through the front door, their faces red like they had run here. I raised an eyebrow at them from the couch.

"You guys okay?" I asked.

"L-Layla," Kacey sputtered out. She held her hand out toward me and in it was a magazine. Neena did the same but with a newspaper.

"Doing some light reading I see," I commented, standing up. They both glared at me, finally catching their breath.

"You are on the cover!" Neena yelled out, coming toward me.

"Wait, what?" Kacey and Neena surrounded me, holding out their magazine and newspaper. I looked down and gasped loudly. They were right; on the front page of the *New York Times* and the *New Yorker* magazine. "What the hell!" I ripped the newspaper out of Neena's hand and read the little article.

I stood there wide-eyed after reading it. Someone had taken Alex and I's photo when we were on our date, and now it was spread across every newspaper stand in New York. *Great, just great. Now another thing I have to worry about.*

"So, you went on the date with Alex I see," Neena said sarcastically. I held back a glare. Now was not the time.

"How did this happen?" Kacey asked, pulling the

paper from my tight grip. The edges were bent.

"I don't know. I didn't see anyone with a huge camera taking pictures of us. There were only a few others there with us." I slumped down on the couch. Who had seen this? "How long has this been out?" I asked, suddenly standing back up. I watched both of them looking at each other and practically having a conversation without me. "Well!"

"Since Saturday morning," Kay said softly while looking closely at me. It'd been out for two days and I hadn't heard about it!

Did this mean Ashton had seen it? Alex? What was I going to do? I was starting to have a panic attack, and my breathing hitched in my lungs.

"Layla, breathe! It's okay!" Kacey said, jumping up and putting her hands on my shoulders. I hadn't had a panic attack in years, and I had forgotten how bad they were. My lungs were closing up, my body was shaking, and my head started pounding, my vision going fuzzy. I looked at Kacey with wide eyes, trying to take a breath. I barely heard Kacey telling Neena to grab a bag from the kitchen, and her practically shoving it at Kacey. She grabbed my shaky hands from my sides and brought them up to grab the bag. With her help, the bag was put against my mouth and I breathed into the bag. Slowly, my lungs started to open up and I could take deep breaths. My body still shook, but my head was clearing up. I felt two pairs of arms lightly grabbing my shoulders and guiding me to the couch.

After about five minutes of breathing into the bag, I was able to pull it away and breathe better. I clenched my shaky hands together, focusing on calming my body down. Neena and Kacey stood by, anxiously waiting for me to be okay. When I shot them a small thankful smile, they finally slumped their tense shoulders and gingerly sat next to me.

"You okay?" Neena asked, almost whispering.

"Y-yeah I am okay." I choked out. "It's just a surprise I guess. And who knows if Ashton or Alex have seen it."

"Well, has any of them contacted you yet?" Kacey asked. I shook my head. No one had, and it was already Sunday afternoon.

"I know this isn't the best time, but who did you choose? I gotta say Alex's date looks pretty fun and sweet," Neena asked, changing the topic.

"It was fun. We ice skated for a while then went and got something to eat before he dropped me off here. Alex is perfect, but…" I trailed off. Both Kacey and Neena had made their feelings about Ashton quite clear, and I kind of didn't want to get yelled at for picking Ashton.

"But nothing compared to Ashton," Kacey finished for me. I nodded and hung my head.

"It doesn't matter, though. He is with someone else now," I said bitterly.

"He's with someone? Since when?" Kacey asked, surprised. "I was just with Nick and he never mentioned Ashton was with anyone." Neena looked at me, waiting for me to tell the story they sensed that had happened.

"Well, my date with Alex was great. He was so sweet, and we had a blast getting to know one another, but when he kissed me, I didn't feel anything. Yeah, it was good, but not like with

Ashton." I reached a hand up and touched my lips, almost feeling them tingle. "I thought about both of them and what I felt, and I choose Ashton. I know I haven't known him that long, and only a month or so isn't enough time to fall for someone, especially someone as aggravating as him, but I have."

"Anyways, yesterday morning I got up later than I wanted, so I booked it to get ready and headed to his apartment. It was pouring out, and the stupid taxi driver practically shoved me outside when we got there. So, I was soaking wet by time I made it to his door. I knocked, and his girlfriend Natasha opened the door in nothing but his shirt. She was the girl he was with at the gala too," I added. "I heard him in the background call her 'babe' and considering the way she looked, I know they are together. So, I left," I finished, slumping down into the couch.

Now, hearing it, I should have stayed and busted through the door, demanding what Natasha was doing there but like with everything else, I was too chicken to do it and ended up leaving. That was what I did, though. If anything got too hard or complicated, I run, never having the guts to stay and work it out or to actually say what I want to say.

"Oh, Lay," Kacey said softly, patting my shoulder. Before her or Neena could say anything else, I sat up and held up my hand.

"I don't want to talk about him anymore. What's done is done and I need to move on." I sent them a look and continued. "I have been all wrapped up in my own drama I don't even know what is going on with you guys. Neena, how is Liam doing?" I asked, taking all the attention off of me. Thankfully they both understood and dropped it all. I knew they would only drop it for so long before they demanded more information or told me their own feelings about the matter.

"Well...he asked me out!" Kacey gasped, and I had to hold back a grin. "Friday night, as I was about to leave the office, he came to a stop in front of me. He looked so yummy in his black slacks and a pretty blue button-up shirt that I almost jumped him then and there, but I was still angry at him. Anyways, we stood there staring at each other before he finally spoke. It was so cute because he was all nervous, but he finally asked me out. Of course, I made him wait for my answer for a few minutes before saying yes. And last night we went on our first date.

"It was amazing! He took me to a fancy restaurant that had great food, and there we talked about basically everything, and afterwards we went and walked through Central Park. It was cold from the rain, so he gave me his jacket which was so sweet. And under the stars he finally kissed me." Neena sat there, swooning from the memory. "It was just great. We have been texting all day, and I think we are going to go out tomorrow night after work."

"That's so sweet," both Kacey and I said at the same time. I had to hold back a triumphant yell. What Neena didn't know was that on Thursday I had to get something from Liam at work, so while he was getting me the records for a client, I asked him about what was happening between him and

Neena. After hearing how much he really liked her but wasn't sure she would say if he asked her out, I basically told him to grow a pair and ask her out. Of course, I knew she would say yes. Liam just needed a little shove to do it. I was glad he finally took my advice and asked her. From the gleaming look in her eyes, I knew she was falling for him.

I should have taken my own advice and asked Ashton out myself, but as I've said before, I'm too stupid and chicken to do so. I turned to Kacey this time, wanting to hear about her love life. Hearing about how other people's love lives were going instead of my nonexistent one helped. It got my mind off of Ashton and Alex for the time being.

"Nothing interesting is going on really," Kacey said, shrugging.

"Boo, you're boring!" I said, sticking my tongue out at her.

"Hey! Nick and I are just taking things slowly. We both like where we are at the moment, and since we were busy all week, we haven't really seen much of each other. I was only with him for a few moments today before seeing the magazine with you, then coming straight here." I couldn't help but feel bad that I had ruined the only time she had seen Nick this week. I had only briefly met Nick, but I knew he liked her almost as much as she liked him. Whenever she would talk about him, like now, her face lit up and her eyes seemed to sparkle. I knew about his playboy ways, but it seemed he had changed since he met Kacey and I was glad. She liked him, and I wouldn't let him break her heart.

Knowing that my friends love lives were going

great made me sad that mine was in shambles. If only mine could be as simple as theirs. It didn't take long for silence settle between us and my mood to dampen.

"You need to tell Alex." Kacey finally said what her and Neena probably have been holding in for a while. I sighed, knowing I have to but I didn't want to. I didn't want to break his heart. I nodded at her and looked down at my hands. The sooner I did it, the better. With a deep breath, I heaved myself off the couch and toward my phone on the counter. Before I could chicken out, I typed a quick message to him.

To: Alex
From: Layla
Hey. Can you meet me at the coffee shop a few doors down from my apartment?

I didn't know how things went from happy to serious in just a matter of minutes. I was hoping that Kacey and Neena would have kept me occupied for a while so I wouldn't have to do this today, but apparently, that wasn't going to happen. I had to face this head-on and on my own. Alex texted me back a minute later agreeing to meet me in five minutes.

"Layla, it is going to be fine. Just tell him what you feel, and I know he will understand. You can't help who you love." Neena nodded behind her, and I shot them a smile. I was thankful they are okay with my decision and were here to cheer me up.

"And afterwards come back here and we will get

good and drunk," Neena added. I laughed and shook my head.

"We got work tomorrow," I reminded her before I headed to get dressed.

I quickly got dressed in a pair of old jeans and an undershirt before sliding on a hoodie. Pulling on a pair of Converse, I brushed my hair into a ponytail and left. There was no use getting all dressed up for what I was about to do. Leaving the apartment, I waved at my friends and smiled when they wished me good luck. I slowly walked downstairs, taking my bottom lip between my teeth trying to think of something to say. I had never done something like this before. In all honesty, Alex was only the third guy I had been with. With no experience dumping someone, I wanted to go the route where I didn't hurt him but I knew there was no other way.

Coming to a stop in front of the coffee shop a few doors down from my place, I took a few deep breaths before walking in. The lovely smell of coffee surrounded me. I glanced around the small shop before coming to a stop at Alex sitting at a table in the back with two cups of coffee already. He stood up and sent me a big smile as I walked toward him with heavy legs. *Oh god, I really don't want to do this.*

"Hey," he said, leaning down and kissing my cheek.

"Hey," I replied softly, taking a seat across from him. "Sorry I'm late."

"No, you're fine. I was a bit early, so I decided to get us some coffee. Do you like sugar?" I nodded and he passed me a cup. "So, I take it you want to talk about something with me," Alex said, breaking the awkward tension.

"How did you know?"

"Well, someone doesn't really call someone at such a short notice and tell them to meet them somewhere if they didn't have something to say." Butterflies swarmed in my stomach as I stared at Alex's face. I looked at his pretty green eyes staring down at me almost in worry, the slight stubble starting to appear on his jawline, and his blonde hair messy like he just got out of bed. Taking a sip of my coffee to calm my nerves, I finally spoke.

"Alex, I'm sorry, but I…can't go out with you anymore," I choked out. "It's not that I don't like you, cause. I do I just…" I trailed off.

"You like someone else," he stated, staring at me. I gulped and nodded, peeking up from under my lashes to see his expression. I thought I would see his face crumpled with hurt, but instead, he looked oddly calm. I looked at him head-on, surprised by his reaction.

"How did you know?" I asked, surprised.

"I didn't know at first, but on Friday night after I kissed you I knew. You kind of just smiled at me then went inside." I folded my hands in front of me, feeling bad. I hadn't realized I did that. "Layla." He reached his hand over the table and put it on top of mine. "I am not mad, really. I am just sorry that I'm not that guy."

"I am so sorry, Alex," I said, feeling my eyes start to fill with tears. "I wish you were too. I really do. You deserve someone who can give you their whole heart, not just a piece. You're amazing, and I hope we can still be friends."

"Of course, we can still be friends. Even if we aren't involved, I would still love your company." He shot me a smile and I returned it with a watery one of my own. "I think I know who the other guy is, just…don't let him hurt you, okay? If he does, I'll kick his ass for you." I laughed at his last sentence.

"Don't worry. My best friend has already said the same thing. He's just…complicated." I trailed off.

"I know, just be careful, okay?" Alex said, squeezing my hands.

"I will, Alex. Thank you for understanding, and I am so sorry again."

"Don't be. When it isn't right, it isn't right." He looked at his watch and back up at me. "I better get going. I have a few things to do." He stood up and I got up with him. We walked out the door together and stood facing one another. "Call me if you ever need anything, and don't forget to text me still. If you want to hang out anytime, I will be there. I'll talk to you soon." He wrapped his long arms around me, and I stood on my tippy toes, wrapping my arms around his neck.

We stood there hugging for a few minutes before pulling apart. With a small kiss on my forehead, he headed to his car and sent me one last wave. I waved back and turned around. As I walked those few feet to my apartment and up the stairs, I felt lighter than I had in a while.

Chapter 11

Layla

When my alarm starting blaring at 5:30 a.m. the next morning, I was so close to breaking the damn thing. Last night, Neena had stayed over until eleven or so having a girls' night, and it wasn't the greatest idea considering all three of us had work early in the morning. At the time, it was fun and a good idea, but now, as I listened to my alarm, I wanted to take it back. I slammed my hand on the snooze button and cracked open my eyes to stare at the ceiling, dreading going to work today.

Knowing I had to see Ashton today, I wasn't all too happy. With a loud groan, I pulled my covers off and stumbled into the bathroom scrubbing my tired eyes. The day hadn't even started and I had a feeling it was going to be a long one. I washed my face, and put a little bit of makeup on before brushing my wavy hair. Going to my closet, I pulled out a new pretty orange dress, and since it had thinner straps, I also put on a cute black blazer. I pulled it on before going to the mirror. The dress hugged my body but wasn't too slutty or fancy for work, and the black blazer helped make it look more professional. Sliding on my black heels, I grabbed my bag and phone and left the apartment.

When I got to work, I said my hellos to everyone, including Judy. Opening my office door, I was met with a pile of paperwork. *Got to love Mondays,* I thought sarcastically. With a sigh, I set my stuff down and got to work. I honestly didn't know how all this work was able to pile up on my desk since Friday night. I only left about twenty minutes earlier than most days; like that was enough time for all this to happen. I spent the next little while slowly making my way through the pile. I knew that if someone honestly asked Ashton how good of a PA I was, I bet he would say I sucked, and I'd kind of agree.

I mean, yeah, I do the work I am assigned and at first, I went to the meetings with Ashton, but lately, I hadn't been doing so. I had been avoiding him at almost every cost, and in doing so I hadn't gone to any meetings or even stayed later to discuss some of the paperwork and reports. Thankfully, today time seemed to go fast and I was holed up in my office until lunch came around. I knew that if I saw Ashton, I would break down and probably do something I would regret later. I mean, it was basically somewhat my fault, but still.

The clock hit noon, and I only had a few things left to do, so I decided to head to the cafeteria and meet up with Neena and Liam. I walked quickly past Ashton's door, but at the same time slow enough where Judy wouldn't think I was being weird. My heels clicked against the tile as I walked toward the cafeteria. Not really in the mood for anything to eat, I went straight to the Frappuccino machine to get some much-needed coffee. If I was going to make it the rest of the day, I would definitely need a pick-me-up.

Once my drink was done, I turned and looked around the room trying to spot Neena and Liam. Just as I was about to give up, I spotted them in a corner booth sitting close to one another and laughing about something. I was torn between going over and interrupting them or to go back upstairs, I decided to let them be and was about to turn away when I heard Neena yell my name. Turning around, I walked over to their booth and shot them a guilty look.

"Sorry, I didn't want to interrupt you guys."

"No, you're fine," Liam said, nodding to the other side of the booth. I slid in then took a sip of my drink, watching them. Liam grinned down at Neena, who was curled up on his side, I stared at them, feeling jealous and sad. I wish someone would look at me like that, like I was their entire world. Smiling softly at them, I grinned inside of my mind knowing I helped get them together. At least I could help other people's love lives. The longer I sat there, the more I felt like a third wheel and like I was ruining their moment together.

"I better go," I said, standing up, but they didn't seem to notice what I said and kept talking. Rolling my eyes, I walked away. I figured I might as well get back to work instead of just trying to kill time.

The more occupied I was, the faster the clock would move.

About two and a half hours later, I leaned back in my chair and rubbed my head. My eyes were burning from having to stare at the computer for a long time, and my hand ached from all the writing I had to do. I closed my eyes, feeling proud of myself for getting that whole pile done. Not even after a minute of congratulating myself, my work phone decided to buzz.

"Hello?" I spoke into the phone, keeping my eyes closed.

"Ms. Kingston?" a female voice asked.

"Yes, this is she."

"This is Karen Fielding, the head coordinator in human resources."

"Oh, hello," I answered sitting up. They'd never called me in person before, so something must be wrong.

"I hate to bother you, but there is a slight problem with that paperwork you sent to us Friday. My workers hadn't caught it, but I was going over the file and saw it does not have a signature."

"A signature?" I asked, confused. I knew what file she was talking about, but I hadn't known that it needed a signature.

"Yes, a signature by Mr. Miller." I rubbed the bridge of my nose, trying not to groan. That file needed to be filed and out by Friday night. It was all the paperwork on our newest client and one of the wealthiest ones to invest in us. I couldn't screw up this file.

"Okay, just a signature is needed?"

"Yes, and any other changes that he wants made to it," Karen said. "I need it back here by five o'clock tonight." A string of curse words ran through my head when I said a thank you and hung up.

Okay, it was almost 3:30, so I had about two hours until I needed it back. *I can do this,* I thought to myself. I quickly left my office and headed downstairs to the human resources level. Asking around, I finally found Karen's office and got the file back. My heels clicked loudly as I walked off the elevator and toward Ashton's office.

"Hey, Judy. Is Ashton in?" I asked. Hopefully, I could quickly get Ashton's signature on the form and get it back with plenty of time to spare.

"He isn't, actually. He just stepped out," Judy said. I was looking around the office until she said Ashton was out and my eyes snapped to her.

"Wait? He's gone? Where did he go?" I asked.

"I don't know. He just said he was leaving and wouldn't be back." *No, no, no. This can't be happening.*

"He didn't say where he was going?"

"Sorry, sweetie, no." Great, now I have to run all over New York trying to find him for a damn signature. I wanted to yell but instead, I bit my lip.

"It's okay. Thanks though." I headed to my office to see if I could get a hold of him. I dialed his number and held my phone between my shoulder and neck while I went through the file. I wanted to make sure I did it right, especially if I had missed getting Ashton's signature.

The annoying voicemail voice entered through

my phone. I tapped my finger against the desk, waiting impatiently so I could leave a message.

"Hey, Ashton, it's Layla." Right after I said it, I wanted to slap myself. *Of course, Ashton knows it's you, Layla.* "I really need you to call me back, okay? So, when you get this, please call me. It's very important." I ended the call and stared down at the phone almost like I was trying to make it ring with my mind. *I'll give him a few minutes then I'll call again.*

I leafed through the file, going over everything. I thought back to the one time Ashton had talked to me last week when he handed me this file.

"I need you get this file all worked out and give it to human resources immediately. It is our new client, and the latest it can go out is Friday. Don't screw this up."

I remembered it specifically because I wanted to strangle him as he walked out of my office. When I had re-gone over the file, I decided that was enough time and called Ashton again. I watched the clock as the hands went around and around more time passing. I got his voicemail again, and I had to grip the edges of my desk so I wouldn't hurl my phone across the room.

"Ashton, it's me again. This is pretty urgent, and I need you to call me immediately. Please," I added before hanging up once again. I couldn't help but think of the irony at the moment; I was Ashton's personal assistant and I was supposed to know where he was at all times but I had no idea. The clock ticked on, and soon five minutes had passed. My body was full of sudden nerves as I thought about what would happen if I didn't get this file in before five o'clock. I tried Ashton's phone one last time, but got nothing again. Instead of leaving a message, I slammed my phone on the counter. *There has to be another way to find Ashton or to get another signature.*

When Ashton had told me not to screw this up, I had caught the warning underneath his tone that if I didn't do this I would have to pay. I sent Ashton what had to be the hundredth text in the last minute. When another five minutes had passed and he hadn't replied, I thought screw it. I grabbed my things and the file before leaving my office. The only place I could think he would be at was his apartment. I quickly made my way to the elevator and to the curb to hail a cab. Sliding inside of one, I told the driver Ashton's address and while we drove to his place, I looked down at my phone practically willing it to ring. I wasn't looking forward to going to Ashton's apartment because of what happened the last time I went, but I had no choice.

"We are here, miss," the driver said, breaking me out of my thoughts.

"Thank you." Handing him the money, I got out and headed inside. As I rode the elevator up, I prayed he didn't have Natasha over again; if he did, I thought I would lose it. *Layla, all you have to do is get his signature and then you can leave.* The elevator doors opened, and I took a deep breath before heading toward Ashton's door. I knocked on the door and waited for an answer. *He better be here,* I thought. When no one answered, I tried again but with the same result. Not having time to do this, I punched in the code and opened the door.

"Ashton?" I called out walking to the living room. Setting my bag, the file, and my black blazer on the couch, I headed toward the kitchen calling out Ashton's name again. Looking around, I didn't see Ashton and started up the stairs toward his bedroom. As I came to the half-open door, I heard voices.

"Ash, baby," a female voice said. *That doesn't sound like Natasha; she doesn't have an accent.*

"No, Allie, I can't," I heard Ashton say. Curiosity got the better of me, so I tried to quietly walk toward the door. Peeking my head around the corner, I saw Ashton turned halfway toward me with a very pretty blonde in front of him. I could only see a little of her, but saw she was wearing a tight black dress that barely went to the top of her tan thighs, a pair of studded heels, and her blonde hair was long and wavy down her back. Ashton had taken off his suit jacket and rolled up his button up shirt to his elbows.

"No, Ash, you still want me." The girl practically purred, running her hand down the front of his chest. From here, I could see Ashton's jaw clenched and his eyes narrowed. When her hands trailed down his chest, I saw his neck vein popping out like he was restraining from doing something.

"Allie, you need to stop." *Allie? Who the hell is Allie?* I watched as she stepped up to him and pressed against him. He grabbed her arms and pushed her away from him.

"Does this have to do with that brunette girl I have been seeing around you? Do you love her?"

149

The girl Allie suddenly narrowed her eyes at Ashton. My eyes widened.

"Layla is none of your concern." Ashton spoke in a deep, threatening tone. If I were in front of him, I would be shaking with how scary his expression was.

"Layla, that's the slut's name?" I couldn't stop the "Hey" that burst from my lips before it was too late. Both of their heads whipped to my direction. I felt my cheeks turning red, and feeling self-conscious from their gazes, I stood up and smoothed down my dress. I held my head up and walked through the door, trying to act like their narrowed eyes didn't bug me. Seeing Allie standing so close to Ashton in what could only be called as a long tube top, caused a sudden a wave of anger washed over me.

"Who are you calling a slut? Have you had a good look in the mirror lately?" I heard myself saying in a tone I'd never used before. It sounded low and almost dangerous, and it surprised me as well as them both. I watched as her eyes widened before narrowing once more on me.

"Layla." She spit out my name like it was poison. "So, this is who you've been screwing while I've been gone." Before I could snap a reply, Ashton beat me to it.

"While you were gone?" he almost boomed. "You cheated on me, stole my money, and left for four years!" Ashton yelled. Suddenly, the pieces fell into place. This was the girl who had broken Ashton and made him the way he is. *She cheated on him and then stole his money?* I felt closer to Ashton in that moment because we both had been cheated on, but his was worse than mine. How could she have stolen money from him then just leave? I took a step closer to Ashton while glaring at Allie.

The anger I felt at Ashton for not telling me and for letting something like this ruin what could have happened between us was building inside of me, but the anger I felt toward Allie was even greater. Yes, Ashton had been a dick to me, but I had seen the good sides of him and this girl was the one to take away the way Ashton used to be. *She just used him for money. Played his feelings like an instrument.*

"You need to leave. You are not welcome here," I stated, the tension in the air wrapping its claws around all three of us.

"Excuse me, but I belong here more than you do. Just because Ashton is fucking you doesn't mean you mean something to him," Allie said to me.

"You are only back here because you need more money, am I right? So, he may be 'fucking' me, but at least I haven't stolen from him. So, take your ass outside and let the door hit you on the way out," I said in a sweet tone.

"Leave before I get security up here to force you to leave," Ashton said next to me. When both Ashton and I glared at her, her eyes kept going back and forth between us two. With a huff and a scream, she stormed past me, knocking her shoulder forcefully into mine. I stood tense beside Ashton until I heard the front door slam shut, and I let out the breath I didn't know I was holding. That was actually a lot easier than I expected. I thought she would have put up more of a fight, but that, of course, didn't mean she will go away so easily. I felt Ashton next to me let out a long breath.

"Layla—" he started, but I whirled around to face him. My anger toward him was now starting to surface.

"Don't you even start, Ashton," I hissed out. "This is why you couldn't answer my calls or texts?"

"What? I came home to grab something and she appeared at my door. We had barely started talking when you interrupted."

"Interrupted? I just helped you and that's all I get, that I interrupted! I got her to leave." I barely contained my anger. I'd never wanted to yell so bad my entire life.

"I was handling it just fine. You don't know anything about the situation," Ashton hissed back at me, taking a step forward.

"You're right I don't! I don't know shit because you keep it all in! Do you realize that you let her win? You let her break you."

"She did not break me." His eyes narrowed even more, and his jaw was clenched so hard I thought I could hear teeth grinding against each other.

"Yes, she did! You don't think I can see how she has hurt you? You walk around with a shield around yourself, not letting anyone in. She made you this way, didn't she? Cold, heartless, not letting anyone in." I watched as Ashton flinch at those words, but I couldn't stop the words from overflowing. I was finally saying the stuff I had wanted to say for a while.

"That is why you broke it off with me, isn't it?

You think I'm just like Allie, and that I'll do the same thing." Just the idea that he thought I would be the same as his ex hurt more than anything.

"Don't say her name," Ashton all but growled at me.

"Answer my question," I bit out. "Did you break it off with me because you thought I would be just like her?" I didn't need his answer because his expression said it all. His face had always been a mask, showing no emotion until now. Written across his face was guilt, anger, and sadness. Even without words, it felt like a blow to the stomach. Swallowing back the tears threatening to spill, I clenched my jaw and turned to walk away.

"Layla, don't walk away from me," Ashton said, grabbing my hand and whirling me around.

"Don't!" I ripped my hand out of his. I lost my battle with my tears and they started rolling down my cheeks.

"I did it to protect you from me. After what Allie did to me, I haven't cared about anybody besides my family, women especially."

"You can't stand there and make up excuses for what you have done, for what you have said to me!" I yelled through my tears.

"Listen to me." He grabbed my hand again. "From the moment I saw you at that club, I wanted you, more than any woman I have ever wanted. I couldn't get my mind off of you no matter what I did. I couldn't sleep and lay there thinking of your face and your smile every single night. After I asked you out and spent the day with you, I knew I felt something for you. Something stronger than

153

anything I had felt, even for Allie, and she was the first girl I was really in love with. I knew from the way I have treated women that I didn't deserve you, so I ended anything before it could begin."

"Then decided to treat me like shit to make yourself feel better, huh!"

"No, I didn't mean for all of that to come out. I thought the more I pushed you away the better it would be for you. I didn't want you mixed up with me, but it was so hard to do. Layla, you don't know how hard it is not talking to you daily, or kissing you every second of the day. It drove me crazy! Then, right when I decided to tell you how I felt, you had to go and get with Alex Ryder, the one guy I hate with everything I have!"

"Why does it matter I am with Alex? I came here Saturday morning but found you with Natasha! So, don't make this out to be all me! Not even two weeks after you broke it off with me, you showed up to the gala with her on your arm, then kissed her in front of me. Did you not think that would affect me?" Thinking back to that moment my chest hurt.

"Natasha doesn't mean anything to me! Saturday, she broke it off with me saying she doesn't want to stand in the way of anybody else. If I had known you were here, I would have gone to you immediately. And I wasn't thinking! I wanted to get you to move on without me. But I don't want you to! I want you here with me. I want to kiss you anytime I want, to hold you against me, to see you smile up at me, not Alex!" His blue eyes were blazing as he stared down at me.

"You lost that right when you pushed me away

and called me a mistake!" My tears were coming stronger.

"Layla." He stood right up against me, making me take a step back. We continued this until my back hit the wall. He put his hands on either side of my head, trapping me in. "You are not a mistake," he said lowly, looking down into my gray eyes. I tried to look away, but he reached and softly grabbed my chin. "You are *not* a mistake. You arc the best thing to happen to me. I didn't know it until now, when you stood by me with Allie. You are everything I want, you argue with me and make me want to pull my hair out at times, you make me feel like my old self, and you make me want to change," he said softly, tracing his fingers along my jaw.

My eyes threatened to close, but I kept them open staring into Ashton's eyes. I saw the sincerity in them, and something else I couldn't make out. The way he was staring down at me I felt my body heat up and emotion flare inside of me. I wanted him so badly.

"I want you all to myself," he whispered, lowering his head to my ear. I shivered and felt goosebumps trail up and down my bare arm.

His hands lowered, and he slowly ran them down my arms until he reached my hands. I could feel my body heating up, and I licked my lips. His fingers were through mine. When I was distracted by his gaze, he left my arms up and above my head, holding them in place. His hot breath tickled my face as he leaned in closer. I finally closed my eyes as his lips captured mine. He didn't kiss me softly; instead, he kissed me with what seemed like everything he had.

It was a hard and demanding kiss. He kept my wrists together with one hand while bringing the other one at an agonizing pace down my neck, down the side of my breast and to my waist before gripping it and pulling me roughly toward him. I couldn't stop my body from arching into his hard chest while kissing him back. I put everything I had into it, wanting him to feel everything I felt. When we were kissing, everything seemed to fade away and it was only us two. I forgot about all of our problems and focused on his lips against mine and his warm hand on my waist.

Ashton's lips became more demanding, and his tongue made its way into my mouth. I couldn't help but moan low in my throat and press even more against him. My moan must have set something off inside of him because he let go of my hands and gripped my waist with both hands, lifting me up. I wrapped my legs around his waist, and he led us to his bed. He dropped me suddenly on the bed, forcing our lips apart and a squeal to escape my lips as I bounced on the bed. Before I was even settled on the bed, Ashton was on top of me in-between my legs. He kept his weight off of me by having his forearms on either side of my head.

I wrapped my legs around his waist, and ran my fingers up his face and jaw before going to his hair. It was just as I remembered, soft as silk. His lips landed on mine again, and I softly bit his bottom lip. With a growl, he kissed me harder and pressed me into the bed further. My body felt like it was on fire, and my hands left his hair and gripped the front of his shirt. My fingers made quick work of his buttons, and soon I was peeling it off of his upper body. My hands trailed down his muscular back, and I dug my nails in when he let go of my lips and starting kissing and sucking my neck.

"Ashton," I moaned. He took my hint and reached his hand behind my back, slowly unzipping my dress. After he had it off, I unbuttoned his pants and pulled them down and off his legs.

I lay naked beneath him, feeling self-conscious knowing he would be seeing my scar. It was the thing I hated the most and I hated showing it to people. I looked up at Ashton under my lashes to see his reaction. His face was clear of emotion, and I felt his finger run across it. I shivered and looked up fully at him. He leaned down and kissed me so hard taking my breath away and almost saying he didn't mind it. He looked down at me and sent me a look to ask if I was ready. With a nod and a smile, he spread my legs before plunging inside of me. I gasped and arched my back gripping his hair. We spent the rest of the night in bed together, forgetting everything but us.

Chapter 12

Layla

I woke up the next morning to something heavy draped across my stomach and warm air being blown against my neck. I cracked open my eyes and waited for them to adjust before glancing around. As I looked around the room that wasn't mine, I remembered what had happened yesterday. I looked down at the arm across my bare stomach and followed it up to Ashton's sleeping face. The covers were bunched around his waist, leaving both of our tops bare. Ashton was laying on his front with his heavy arm out, keeping me held down and pressed against him.

Looking at him while he slept, I couldn't help the smile that formed across my face. He looked so peaceful and almost innocent, and that seemed to make him cuter in my eyes. His face was always like a brick wall, and his jaw always clenched, but when he slept, it relaxed and smoothed out. I reached out my one arm that wasn't trapped to my side and moved a stray hair that had fallen across his forehead. I thought about last night and felt my body warm at the thought.

Last night was just…great. Ashton made me feel so safe and loved while at the same time like an animal. It had been a while for me, and Ashton made sure to be gentle with me at first. The last thing I remembered about last night was coming down from my high and feeling Ashton kiss me softly on the lips before falling asleep. Probably not the nicest thing falling asleep on him, but being wrapped in his arms I felt myself drifting off. It was the best night sleep I have gotten in a long while.

As gently as I could, I moved his heavy arm off of my stomach and sat up placing it where I just was. I looked around and spotted his button up shirt I had thrown on the floor last night. Quickly getting up not to bother Ashton, I grabbed his shirt and buttoned it up. Missing being near him, I got back in bed. I reached a hand out and traced my fingers in some random design across his muscular back, which was still a little red from when I had run my nails down it. I couldn't help but blush at my actions. I looked around the room, taking in everything with almost different eyes. The question of how many girls he has had in this room nagged at my mind, but I pushed it back for the moment. Later, when Ashton got up, he was going to be bombarded with questions, and he better have some good answers. Last night was great and all, but we had a lot to work out before I could even think of trusting him, especially with my heart.

Looking down at his back, I noticed a little

below his shoulder blade was a small scar that looked like it was made by glass or something. I ran my finger over it, wondering what happened there. I thought about my own scar. Ashton's reaction last night surprised me. I thought he would look at it in disgust, but instead, he ended up running his finger against it and kissed it. He had looked up at me briefly, sending me a look that said I would be explaining later before his mouth traveled lower. Then, of course, I lost my entire train of thought the rest of the night.

I was busy in my own thoughts, my finger still running over his little scar, when a deep voice filled with sleep spoke to the side of me.

"Nick did that," Ashton said. I looked down and saw he had his head turned to face me on the pillow, his blue eyes staring up at me.

"Sorry, I didn't mean to wake you," I said, almost whispering.

"That's okay. I liked you running your fingers on my back." He shot me a grin and a little wiggle of his eyebrows. I laughed and shook my head at him.

"So, Nick did this?" I asked, bringing the subject of his scar.

"Yeah, we were seventeen at the time, and were play-wrestling in my living room" He brought his hands up and put them under his head while I traced the edge with my finger tip. I saw him shiver slightly before going on with his story. I felt a little giddy inside knowing I could make him shiver by my touch. "I had pinned him down more times than he did me and it was making him mad. It was my fault because I told him to take his best shot at me, feeling cocky. He suddenly came at me while I was distracted, hitting my straight in my stomach and the next thing I knew, I was falling on my mother's glass coffee table. When I landed on it, one of the glass shards embedded itself in my shoulder. I didn't notice it because I was so busy thinking of all the ways my mother was going to kill me. Anyways, I had to go to the hospital and get stitches even though it still scarred."

"I bet your mom was pissed," I said, smiling at his story.

"Let's just say I ended up getting grounded. Yes, at seventeen I was grounded, and Nick and I were told to never wrestle in the house again," Ashton said, laughing.

"Nick must have felt terrible."

"He did. The entire way to the hospital, he said sorry to me at least fifty times before I told him to shut up. I, of course, forgave him because it was basically my own fault I did tell him to do his best."

"Sounds like you and Nick got in a lot of trouble together."

"Tons. We were wild teenagers." He grinned at the thought. "So, does my scar make me hotter?" he asked with a smirk and a wiggle of his eyebrows.

"Oh yeah, it's very sexy," I said sarcastically and rolled my eyes. When I rolled my eyes, I caught sight of the alarm clock on the bedside table and gasped. 9:45.

"Ashton, we have work!" I yelled and jumped up off the bed. I ran around the room gathering my clothes in my arms while Ashton turned and sat up in bed. Seeing him in bed shirtless and only a sheet covering him made my body warm, but I ignored him and whipped my head around trying to find my shoes.

"Layla. Layla!" Ashton yelled. I looked at him but still kept glancing from the corner of my eyes for the rest of my clothes. "I already called in. We aren't going to work today."

"You did?"

"Yes, I got up earlier and called Judy saying neither of us would be coming in." I dropped everything in my arms and my eyes widened at the mention of Judy, remembering the real reason I came here yesterday. The file!

"Shit, shit, shit, shit!" I chanted and reached up to grab my hair. I touched it then pulled my hand away, feeling all the knots that were in it. Of course, I look like shit and Ashton looks like he came off of the runway.

"What's wrong?" Ashton asked, grabbing a sheet and wrapping it around himself before coming toward me.

"I had a file I needed you to sign yesterday, and it had to be in to human resources before five last night." I groaned.

"Layla, it's okay. I'm the head of the company. Remember, it can be late," he said, reaching for my chin and bringing up so my eyes met his. "Plus, there is no way I'm letting you out of my sights today, especially if you're dressed like that." He let go of my chin, and I looked down at his shirt barely covering me. It was to maybe mid-thigh and a few buttons were undone. As I looked down at myself, I remembered seeing Natasha just like this only two days ago. With that thought in mind, I had to reluctantly move away from Ashton. Before anything else could happen between us, I needed to know Ashton wasn't going to run off to Natasha again, that he wouldn't just sleep with me then push me away again, and that he was actually serious about me. I couldn't get my heart broken because of him again.

"What's wrong?" he asked, looking down at my face. Keeping my gaze away from his nicely toned abs, I took a deep breath knowing I was about to ruin our little peace bubble.

"We need to talk…you know, before things go any further," I said, and as soon as the words left my lips, I thought this sounded like Ross and Rachel from *Friends* when they get back together the first time.

"Okay, I agree," Ashton said, surprising me. I stared at him, surprised. I was waiting for him to get mad or say I was crazy for wanting to talk.

"Wait, did you just say you agree with me?" I asked, dumbfounded.

"Yes, I did. Is that surprising?" he asked, smiling softly down at me, tucking a strand of my hair behind my ear. I nodded, still surprised he didn't put up a road block for me. "Layla, I want to show you how serious I am about this, about our relationship. I will do anything to get you to forgive me and let me be with you." I held back a swoon and instead smiled at him.

"Good. Now let me go shower because I feel all gross. And I can't be a good sight to see," I said, pulling away from him.

"You are beautiful either way." Ashton kissed the top of my head and backed away. "Go shower…unless you need some help," he suggested, smirking at me.

"Nope, I think I can do it all by myself," I said, putting extra emphasis on the word "all." With a smirk at the way his blue eyes darkened, I turned to go to the bathroom. A slap on my ass made me yelp and jump, turning to him. He just smirked wider and turned away from me. Shaking my head, I headed to shower.

It took me forever to get the shower started because of all the different knobs it had. There were two knobs for the temperature then a handle bar-like thing; I had no idea what it did. I just tilted it up and the water finally started. When the shower finally warmed up, I stripped and stepped under the water. The shower head wasn't like mine at home; it was almost like a waterfall. It fell down on my shoulders softly, and I almost moaned. *I could stay in here forever.*

I washed my hair and body thoroughly, using Ashton's shampoo since he had nothing else. I stood there smelling my arm after using his body wash, and man, did it smell good. Plus, I didn't mind smelling like Ashton. The water started turning cold, so I forced myself to finally get out. Wrapping a towel around me, I wiped away the fog that collected on the mirror and looked at myself.

My brown hair stuck to my face and lay limp and wet down to the middle of my back. My cheeks are a slight pink from the water, but my face seemed to glow. Staring back at me were my gray eyes, and instead of looking dull and almost lifeless, they looked brighter and seemed to shine. If being with Ashton for one day did this to me, I couldn't wait to see what would happen after being with him longer. A knock on the door jerked me out of staring at myself and I called out.

"Come in." The door opened and Ashton stood there, now in a pair of boxers holding what appeared to be a pile of clothes.

"You're finally done," he said, coming more into the bathroom and setting the clothes on the counter.

"Hey, your shower was hard to work and…it's amazing," I added.

"It would have been better if I was there," Ashton said, taking a step closer to me. With him being practically naked around me, I didn't know if I could control myself.

"Nope, back away, pervert. I need to get dressed, so out you go." I put my hands on his hard stomach and tried pushing him out the door. He was like a brick wall. I pushed harder, trying to not let my towel slip off of me at the same time. "Ugh, move, you brick wall!" I grunted. Ashton laughed but finally left the room, closing the door behind him. I stared at it after he left, smiling. If this was how Ashton really was, I liked this better.

Not wanting to take a chance on him coming back in unannounced, I quickly grabbed the clothes he gave me and got dressed. Embarrassed, I picked up my panties on the top and cringed that Ashton grabbed them. I didn't want to wear the same pair, but with no other choice I slid them on and the rest of the clothes, which consisted of a pair of long sweats and a black shirt that had **Green Day** written on it in faded letters. Searching through the cabinets, I finally found a brush before brushing my knotted hair and exiting the bathroom.

Ashton sat on the bed looking down at his phone before looking up at me.

"You look good in my clothes," he remarked. I shook my head at him.

"Go shower." I left the room and headed downstairs. I headed for the kitchen to make us some breakfast while thinking through all the things I wanted to say to Ashton. As I found the stuff to make pancakes and pans, I started on the batter, making a speech inside of my head. It was the writer in me who liked to have it all planned out before saying it. I poured some pancakes in the pan and leaned against the counter.

Layla, just explain how you feel and tell him how much he has hurt you. Then, of course, ask about Allie. I had to know what happened between them in order to make more sense of why Ashton was the way he was. *Then let him explain.* I had the tendency to run off before hearing what people had to say, so this time I was going to force myself to stay put and listen to everything Ashton had to say, whether it hurt or not. I planned on making him apologize multiple times before anything else could happen. I was not going to be a pushover.

Putting the bunch of pancakes I had made on a plate, I grabbed two more before searching for the syrup. Right as I put it on the counter, Ashton walked in wearing a pair of worn holed blue jeans and a light blue shirt that hugged his upper body.

"You cooked," he said, more a statement than a question.

"Yes, I did. Let's eat then talk." He nodded and took a seat.

We ate in silence until we both were full and groaning. As the silence wore on, I played with my fingers on the counter trying to come up with something to say to start the conversation I knew we were both dreading.

"It was four years ago," Ashton said, breaking the silence. I turned and looked at him, listening. "It was my twenty-first birthday, and my parents had let me and Nick have a party at our beach house. We basically invited the entire college, honestly. Allie and I had been dating for two years, and I was completely in love with her, although Nick thought I was crazy since he never liked her from the start. Anyways, I thought long and hard about it and finally decided I was going to propose to her that night at the party." When he said propose, I felt my breath hitch, and jealousy mixed with pain flared inside of me, but I bit it down, still listening to his story.

"I was so young and in love I didn't care that we were only twenty-one, and had one more year to graduate. Allie was everything I had wanted. People use to say we made the best couple and that they could see us getting married one day. Well, I talked to my parents, who finally got on board, and hers before fully committing to it and buying the ring. I had it all planned. I was going to have Nick set up a blanket with candles on the beach down away from all the people, then I would take her there before

167

proposing. I was stupid and blind that I didn't think anything was wrong when I walked in on her in my bedroom, dropping my phone quickly on the dresser. Anyways, the party had more people than I thought would show, and I had lost Allie somewhere along the night.

"The beach was empty besides a few stragglers. I looked for a little bit, asking around for Allie before someone told me they saw her go down the hallway to my bedroom." Ashton stared down at the granite counter clenching his jaw. "When I got there, she was in my bed, half-naked, with Alex Ryder." I felt my mouth drop open. *Alex?* "She...she looked happy that I had caught her, like she had planned the whole thing. Somewhere between me yelling at Alex and tackling him, she fled the room. Nick pulled us apart, but I was too angry so I sent everyone home even though it was only nine. Knowing that Allie was gone, I drowned myself in whiskey while Nick sat beside me watching over me.

"The next morning, my mother called me yelling at me for giving Allie five million dollars. I didn't realize that was what she was doing in my room when I caught her before the party. Afterwards, I called her, texted her, even went to her parents' house, but they were gone. She used me for my money then took off." His voice wasn't angry or cold; it was sad and hollow. *And on his birthday.* Reaching out, I laid a hand on his shoulder. I kind of remember hearing about a big party some popular guy was hosting and how it ended early, but I never went and only briefly heard about it. Guess it was Ashton's party.

"Ashton that's…terrible. That's why you use women, huh?" I asked softly. I understood how he felt, having been cheated on myself. But at least I didn't get stolen from. Yes, it hurt hearing him say how much he loved her and that he was going to propose to her, but hearing the tone of his voice, I knew he felt nothing for her anymore, and hadn't for a long time. He didn't answer me as I rubbed his back. I got why he hated Alex because he was caught cheating with his ex, but I knew Alex wouldn't have done it intentionally. He didn't seem like that type.

"Mine was on my anniversary," I said after Ashton was silent for a while. He looked over at me, confused. "When my boyfriend cheated on me. It was our two-year anniversary when I found him in bed with another girl. He said he would pick me up at six, but after two hours of waiting I went to his dorm to see if something was wrong and instead found him having sex with some slut." I shrugged. It didn't hurt that bad anymore, talking about it. "He's now engaged and I'm happy for him," I added, looking over at Ash. His blue eyes held sympathy but also admiration.

"You don't sound hurt about it," he commented. I shrugged.

"I realized that by holding onto it I only hurt myself. There's nothing I can do to change it, and what happened, happened. I mean, I was hurt for a long time, but I finally got over it. Would I go back and change it? No. Do I wish I never met him and fell in love? No," I stated simply. And it was true; it

169

happened for a reason and I couldn't change the past. "You need to move on from it. I'm not saying forget it completely but instead, acknowledge what happened, let yourself hurt, then move on." I stared into his eyes. "You can't let it keep holding you hostage."

"Do you always know what to say? And be so happy all the time?" he asked.

"Well, yes to the first one." I grinned. "But it took me a *long* time before I could even start to be happy. If Kacey hadn't helped me through everything, I wouldn't be here."

"Everything as in…" I looked at him, asking myself if I was ready to let him know about my dark past. I had learned to accept it, but I didn't know if Ashton would.

"I'm going to tell you something about myself, so please don't run off afterwards," I said, my eyes pleading up into his. He had confusion written across his face, but he slowly nodded. Taking a deep breath, I told him everything about my parents and what they did to me. How they use to beat me on a regular basis, how I had to learn to cover the bruises with Kacey, the things they said to me, and finally my scar. The whole time I talked, I didn't once look up at him, not wanting to see his expression. Just one look from Ashton and I knew I would break down, and I couldn't right now. My voice was emotionless and hollow like his had been the entire time he spoke.

I let out a breath as I finished my story and sat there in silence. I didn't dare look anywhere besides at the counter. For all I knew, I could be talking to an empty chair. It was hard telling someone about my past, and I felt like I was reliving it all again. It had taken a *long* time for me to not be skittish around people, and to go out of my own little protective bubble. I used to hate thinking about the things my parents did to me, but after a few years being away at college, I came to realize that if they hadn't done that to me, I wouldn't be who I was. I would be an entirely different person, and I honestly love who I am. Yes, I hated my parents with a fiery passion, and I was glad I never had to see them again, but I did still ponder what my life would have been like if I had loving parents, parents who I could talk to about anything and hear them say they love me every day. I wouldn't deny that I was insanely jealous of Kacey's relationship with her parents; I wanted that for myself, but in the end, her parents kind of became my own and I realized how stupid my jealousy was.

I'd come to realize that sometimes being blood related meant nothing and having a family who wasn't blood related was everything. Kacey was my sister, and her parents were my parents. We were a family, whether we were blood or not. They said blood was thicker than water, but in some cases, it wasn't, and that was mine included.

I waited with bated breath for Ashton to say something, anything. I wanted to steel myself for his rejection, but I couldn't. After baring my soul to him, I didn't know how I would feel if he rejected me.

"Layla," he finally said, breaking the thick tension. His tone showed nothing as I awaited his words. "You are incredible." *What*—I looked up at him in surprise. He stared down at me with admiration and love instead of pity and disgust. "You went through all of that, and look at the way you are. You didn't let that take you down, and you've become a better, stronger person."

"You're not disgusted with me?" I asked, tears starting to form in my eyes.

"Baby, no." He stood up by me. He grabbed my chair and spun me around until he stood in-between my legs. "You are incredible. You are nothing what your parents told you, at all. You are not worthless, nor ugly, nor are you going to end up alone; I won't allow it. Layla, you are beautiful, smart, sexy, funny, amazing, strong, and completely worth everything in this world.

"If only I could go to parents and beat the shit out of them, your mother included, for ever saying such things to you and hurting you. I wish I could have protected you from all of that, and what I've said to you, I don't expect you to forgive me. I'm no better than your parents. But Layla." He softly cupped my cheeks, looking down at me. "I will spend the rest of my life begging for your forgiveness, proving every single day that you are not worthless and mean the entire world to me. I didn't know what love felt like until I found you and fell deeply in love with you when I didn't even know I had. I tried to push you away, forcing myself not to feel anything toward you, but instead, I ended up falling even more. I don't want your forgiveness, and I don't expect you to give it to me right away, but I will work for it and prove my

172

feelings for you.

"I have done and said some terrible inexcusable things to you, and I will not make that mistake again. Layla, you make me into a better man than I ever thought I could be. I feel whole when I'm near you, I feel happiness inside of me instead of nothing, and I feel as if I can see the gold at the end of a rainbow." I smiled at him while tears leaked out of my eyes and rolled down my cheeks. "I do not want to be the reason you cry anymore. I want to be the one making you smile and laugh." He opened his mouth to talk, but I lifted my hand and placed it over his mouth.

"Ashton, the moment I met you, my life was turned upside down. My life isn't filled with nothing anymore. I have been hurt, happy, confused, sad, and hopeful the entire time I have known you. When I am with you, I don't feel like a screw up or that I'm broken. I didn't want to be with anyone until you came along, and somehow you wiggled your way into my heart. Even when you were a jackass to me, I still liked you. When people would say things about you, I knew that wasn't the real you, because I had seen the real you. Yes, we fight, argue, and hurt each other, but at the end of it all, I will still love you. You make me forget everything my parents have said to me, and you make me feel worth it for once in my life.

"I'm not saying I forgive right at this moment for everything you have done to me, but it is a start. You accept me for me, and I do the same for you. We are a messed-up pair, but we fit together like a jig saw puzzle. This is going to be hard, but I know we can make it work. That is, if you want me," I said, dropping my hand from his mouth. A real full-blown smile bloomed across Ashton's face before he leaned down and captured my lips with his. We kissed until we were forced to come up for breath. He laid his forehead against mine.

"Layla Kingston, I want you forever."

I grinned up at the man I had somehow come to love despite everything we had put each other through. The man who made me feel like a different and better me; someone who wasn't afraid of taking a chance. The man who had somehow fixed my heart without me even realizing it. The man who had captured my entire heart and soul when I didn't think someone could. We had already been through a lot, and I know we will as well in the future, but I knew deep down this was right and I was going to fight for it with everything I had. I was looking at my light at the end of the tunnel, and knowing it was everything I have ever wanted.

I, Layla Kingston, made the cold-hearted playboy feel something inside.

Epilogue Part 1

One year later

"Layla, get your ass home right now!" Kacey yelled through the phone. I quickly pulled it away from my ear, not wanting to go deaf.

"Kacey, why? I still got stuff to do here," I said.

"Have you forgotten it is your one-year anniversary?" she asked.

"No, I haven't." In fact, I'd been looking forward to today all week. Ashton and I decided that our year anniversary would be on the same day as our first date.

"Well then get home so I can help you get ready." With that, Kacey hung up on me. I shook my head, setting my phone on my desk. I grinned down at my screensaver; it was a picture of Ashton and I in London about a month ago. I was grinning at the camera, and Ashton was smiling widely down at me; it had to be my favorite picture of us.

To say this year had been crazy was an understatement. After Ashton and I worked things out, it took a few good weeks before I forgave him, and we became an official couple. I still worked as his PA. His parents were happy we were together; his mother more than his father. And I was pretty close with Ashton's sister, Ariel. We met the weekend after Ashton and I got together to have dinner with his family, and we got to talking and clicked. She was now part of Kacey, Neena, and I's little group.

There was even a cheating scandal that happened when reporters found out I was with Ashton, not Alex. I hadn't realized that people cared so much about Ashton and I's relationship, but apparently, they did. Thankfully, though, after Ashton made a few calls, things settled down and we could be out together without people taking photos of us.

After a few months of dating, Ashton asked me to move in with him, which I did say yes to but only after Kacey threatened to cut all my hair off. I felt bad leaving Kacey by herself, but that didn't last long. As my love life was picking up, so was hers. Her and Nick became an official couple a few weeks after Ashton and me, and two weeks after I moved in with him, Nick asked Kacey to move in with him. I was over the moon for my best friend and her boyfriend. They were perfect for each other, and I couldn't be happier that they were together.

While Kacey and I were happy with our boyfriends, Neena was just as happy with Liam. They were still going strong, even though they were opposites. With Neena being sarcastic and blunt like always, Liam was more of the laid back, quiet until spoken to type. They evened each other out, though.

About a week before Ashton asked me to move in, Liam asked Neena. It was actually weird but cool that all in just a few weeks of each other, we all had moved in with our boyfriends.

Deciding that I better get home before Kacey came here to get me, I logged off of my computer and gathered my stuff. Turning off the lights to my office, I made my way to Ashton's to say bye for now, and to maybe learn what we are doing tonight. He had been very secretive about his plans for our anniversary, and no matter how much begging, bribing, or even kisses, he wouldn't budge. I knocked once before entering his office. He sat behind his desk, his suit jacket sitting on the couch and his light gray shirt rolled up to his elbows.

"Hey," I said, setting my stuff on the couch before heading toward him. He looked up and grinned at me, pushing his chair a little bit away from his desk. I walked to him and softly sat down on his lap smiling back at him.

"Hi. Are you leaving?" he asked, kissing me softly on the lips. Even though it had been a year, I still couldn't get enough of his kisses.

"Yeah, Kay called and demanded I come home so she can get me ready," I said, putting my head on his shoulder. Some would think it was weird that I was still his PA when we are together, but it really wasn't. If anything, work was better and easier now.

"You better go then. If not, she'll come here like last time." I almost laughed, remembering what happened last time I ignored Kacey. She'd wanted me to come out with her, Neena, and Ariel, but I told her I was busy at work. I ignored all of her texts and calls, which was not a good idea. Since I hadn't replied, she came here, somehow knowing what floor I worked on, and started yelling my name across the whole floor until I came out. It was really, really embarrassing, and she wouldn't stop until I agreed to leave and go out with her and the girls. It was those moments I really wondered why I was friends with her. Ashton had come to really know her and knew what she was like.

When they first officially met, Kacey hit him, threatened him, then asked him a million questions. By the end of the night, Ashton's arm was bruised, his voice practically gone from responding to all the questions he'd been asked, with his ego deflated. Now it was funny, but then it was so embarrassing even though Ashton reassured me it was fine.

"Okay, yeah, I better. Are you still not going to tell me what we are doing tonight?" I asked, hoping he would.

"Nope, you're going to have to wait. Now go home and get ready. I'll be there in about thirty minutes or so." With that, he kissed me one more time on the lips. I sighed, getting up and grabbing my stuff.

"See ya soon," I called over my shoulder and left his office. "Goodnight, Judy," I said once I passed her, sending her a wave. She called a goodnight back to me and waved. I'd come to love Judy even more in the last year. She was almost as happy as Ashton's mother when she found out we got together. I finally got to meet her husband Gus officially. I loved watching her and Ashton because she was like his second mom, making sure he ate lunch, or that he didn't stay too long here at the office.

When I reached the lobby, I looked around for Neena but didn't see her. Shrugging, I walked outside and saw Clark standing there waiting for me. I grinned as I walked over to him.

"Hey, Clark."

"Layla," he said with a nod and a smile. Over the last year, Clark and I had gotten to know one another more, and I finally met his wife. She was so sweet and nice, and seeing her and Clark together, I knew they truly loved one another. He looked at her like she was his world, and she did the same. He opened the door for me and I slid in, nodding in thanks. During the ride home, I thought about everything Ashton and I had been through and how my love for him had grown.

Yes, we fought every once in a while, but it usually didn't last long; our longest one was not talking for a day, but at the end of the night we both were apologizing. A year later, Ashton made me feel like my body was tingling, and I felt perfect next to him, like my body was made to fit his. I made the right choice being with him, despite what he had done.

"We are here, Layla," Clark said, interrupting my thoughts.

"Oh, thank you." Sending him a smile, I got out and headed inside bracing myself for the whirlwind of Kacey. Opening the door with my set of keys, I stepped into the apartment and Kacey was there in a second.

"There you are! Let's get going. It's going to

take me forever to get you pretty."

"Thank you so much for the compliment, Kay," I said sarcastically as she pulled me upstairs and to the bedroom.

"Now go shower while I grab the outfit." I tried protesting that I didn't need a shower, but with a hard glare from her, I closed my mouth and went and showered. Not even ten minutes later I emerged wrapped in a towel, with my brown hair hanging around my shoulders.

"You shaved, right?" Kacey asked, not even glancing at me. Not even surprised, I answered with a yes. "Okay, put these on." She handed me a pair of lace red panties and matching strapless bra. With a raised eyebrow, I went back to the bathroom and put them on. For some reason, she was acting weird, or weirder than normal. I came back out partially dressed. "Here you go." She handed me a gorgeous deep red strapless gown. I ran my fingers across the silk and smiled over at Kay.

"Where did you get this?" I asked, staring at it in awe. It was so gorgeous. All of it was red with a few silver studs around the waist. It was kind of like a mermaid style dress, with the bottom flaring at around my calves.

"I didn't get it," was all she said before gesturing for me to change. I dropped the towel then stepped into the material, pulling it up. Kacey came up behind me and zipped me up. I stared at myself in the mirror in front of us and loved the look of the dress. Pulling me to the vanity, Kay started on my hair, lightly curling it than pulling it half up. With a little bit of makeup and eyeshadow, she pulled away to grab a matching pair of red pumps.

"All done," she said, stepping away from me, leaving me to gawk at how pretty I looked.

"Thank you, Kay," I said, hugging her. I pulled away just as Ashton entered the room, looking sexy in his gray suit.

"Wow, don't you look stunning," he said, stepping toward me and wrapping his arms around my waist. I grinned up at him, wrapping my own arms around his neck.

"Well, thank you. You don't look too bad yourself, mister."

"I knew I had great taste." He kissed my forehead before pulling away.

"Good taste? You picked out this dress?" I asked, running my hands down the dress.

"Yes, I did." He grinned.

"You do have great taste." I knew he had to have had help from Kacey, but I didn't say anything.

"We better get going." He reached his hand out and I put mine in it.

"Bye, Kay. Thank you so much," I said, looking over my shoulder at her after grabbing a matching small handbag she must have put together. She stood there grinning widely at us, holding her hands to her heart. *Okay, that's not weird.* With one last smile, I let Ashton pull me out of the apartment and toward the car.

Sliding in the car, I grinned over at him as he pulled away from the curb and drove to wherever we were going. I kept quiet, loving the feeling of his thumb rubbing across my knuckles. A few minutes later, we pulled up to a familiar place but I couldn't really see where we were. I waited as he came around the car to get me, and I grabbed his hand as I got out. I looked ahead and almost gasped at where we were. We stood at the entrance of the aquarium, the place we had our first date.

"No way." I turned to Ashton. He grinned at me before pulling me toward the doors. He held the door open for me, and I walked in looking around at the dark aquarium. "Are you sure we can be here?" I asked.

"Of course. I got permission," Ashton said, grabbing my hand once again and leading me further into the room. As we walked through the tunnel with all the fishes, I smiled at the memory of coming here on our first date and talking about *Finding Nemo*. We walked out of the tunnel and entered an open room that was surrounded by glass fish tanks. The room was dark, but candles were everywhere, lighting it up. Right in the middle, a table was set up with two more candles. Flowers, and two place settings. I walked ahead slowly, taking everything in.

"Do you like it?" Ashton asked behind me. I turned in his direction.

"I...absolutely love it," I breathed. I walked to the table, and Ashton pulled out my seat for me before lifting the cover that was over our plates. I expected to see a fancy dish before me, but instead it was multiple slices of pizza. I laughed, shaking my head, looking at him. He took his seat across from me and shrugged.

"I know how much you love pizza, and figured it would be too much if there were a different meal."

"It's perfect." We sat there eating our romantic pizza, talking about our day and random stuff. After we finished, Ashton suddenly got quiet. "Hey, are you okay?" I asked, reaching my hand over and laying it on top of his.

"Yes, I just…Layla, you do not realize how happy you have made me. You are the best thing that has ever happened to me, and I don't ever want to let you go. This past year has been the best year of my life, and I am so lucky to have someone like you in it. You get along great with my family, and they love you like their second daughter." He took a deep breath. "You are absolutely perfect, and I wouldn't change a thing about you. So…" He stood up and came to my side before slowly going down on one knee. I couldn't help but gasp and put a hand against my mouth.

"Layla, I love you with all of my heart and everything that I have. I know I am not perfect, but you make me perfect; you are the other half of me. Yes, we fight and argue, but I wouldn't have it any other way. You make me want to be a better person. I want to be your happy ever after. So, Layla Kingston, will you marry me?" He pulled out a velvet box and opened it, displaying the biggest diamond ring I had ever seen. Tears ran down my face as I looked between him and the ring.

"Yes! Yes!" I yelled and sobbed out, wrapping my arms around his shoulders, crying into his shoulder. He stood up, carrying me with him pulling my feet off the ground and twirling me around. "Yes, I will marry you," I whispered in his ear. He set me down on the ground and pulled away, grabbing the ring. I held out my shaky left hand, and he slipped it on my ring finger. I stared down at the huge diamond then back up at him. Without any warning, I practically jumped on him, wrapping my arms around his neck, his arms around my waist. I kissed him hard.

***

Seven months later

"Oh my god, you look absolutely incredible!" Neena's voice rang out through the room. I turned around and grinned at her. She walked through the doorway and made her way toward me. I wrapped my arms around her, being careful of the dress and my finely curled hair.

"Please be careful of her hair!" Kacey interjected behind us. I pulled away from Neena and smiled at her. She was wearing the pretty light blue bridesmaid dress, same as Kacey. When we went wedding dress shopping, we had found these gorgeous blue strapless dresses that went perfect with the color scheme of the wedding.

Today was finally my wedding day, May seventeenth. I guess I really shouldn't say finally because we actually put this wedding together in only seven months. Ashton's mom helped plan the entire thing, helping me decide the colors, the cake, the invitations. If it weren't for her, this wedding wouldn't be happening. Neena and Kacey were my bridesmaids, as well as Ariel, Ashton's sister. Kacey was my maid of honor, and of course did my hair and makeup, making me look like a princess.

Stepping away from Kacey helping Neena with her hair, I stared at myself in the mirror. Never in my life had I felt so beautiful. My long brown hair was curled down my back in perfect waves, and a veil clipped onto my head, with it mixing down in my dress. The only jewelry I had on was the exact dolphin necklace Ashton got me on our very first date. It seemed weird to some but it meant a lot to me, and it was my something old. My makeup was natural with darker eyeshadow, making my gray eyes pop, and light red lipstick graced my lips. And my dress was absolutely gorgeous. It was a simple white strapless gown, and the upper half had a small light gray ribbon wrapped around with some rhinestones as well, the top hugging my upper body and the rest flowing down and trailing behind me. I had on a pair of matching white heels, but they couldn't be seen. The moment I saw this dress, I knew it was the one. It was simple yet elegant, just what I wanted.

"Okay, it's time," Clare, Ashton's mother, said, coming into the room. My stomach clenched and my legs felt shaky. For some reason, I was nervous that, when I walked down the aisle, Ashton would run away. Taking a deep breath, I turned away from the mirror and to the four girls standing in front of me.

"Layla, you look stunning," Ariel said, grinning over at me.

"Thank you," I said nervously.

"Here you go." Kacey handed me my bouquet of flowers. It was a mix of orange lilies and yellow roses. The bridesmaids had similar ones; Ariel had just lilies, Neena just roses, and Kacey had lilies with two yellow roses.

"Ready to go?" Clare asked, looking at me. I nodded, feeling butterflies in my stomach.

"It's going to be great, Layla, don't worry," Kacey reassured me, squeezing my hand. With a little bit of confidence, I smiled and nodded.

"Okay, I'm ready." Clare nodded and led the way out of the room. Our wedding was being held at Ashton's parents' beach house. I followed behind all of them as we made our way through the house and to the doors leading outside to the beach. I looked through the window and saw a few of the guests seated.

"Layla, honey, you look breathtaking," Mark, Kacey's father, said, making me tear my eyes away from the window. Since I hadn't invited my parents, I asked Kacey's father if he would walk me down the aisle.

"Okay, let's go," Clare said one more time, stepping out and nodding to the orchestra that was going to play the wedding march. Mark weaved his arm through mine and grabbed my hand. I shot Neena and Kacey a small smile before they met up with their men. With one last deep breath and a smile to Mark, we stepped through the door and walked toward the altar.

The sun licked my exposed skin, and a very light breeze washed over me. One of the photographers we hired walked alongside, snapping endless photos. We hired three photographers so one could take pictures at the altar, one on the side as I walked, and another who would stand in the back. We rounded the corner, and I saw all the guests standing and staring in my direction. I ignored their stares as I caught sight of Ashton waiting for me at the altar. He was dressed in a traditional black tux, his brown hair slicked back but still a little messy, just how I liked it. I watched as his face lit up, his eyes running all over my body.

I didn't hear the orchestra playing, or the sounds of the guests whispering over my appearance; instead, I focused fully on Ashton and his face. Seeing him standing there waiting anxiously for me, I felt a small weight lift off of my shoulders. *He is still here. Mark* and I finally reached the altar, and he leaned down and kissed my cheek, grinning at me before handing me to Ashton, who had his hand waiting for mine. I handed Kacey my bouquet before grabbing Ashton's hands.

He pulled me to stand where I was supposed to, in front of him, holding both of my hands in his. Smiling at him, I briefly heard the minister saying the things he had to say until I felt Ashton softly tapping my fingers; it was time for the vows. Taking a deep breath, I said mine.

"You know me better than anyone else in this world, and somehow you still manage to love me. You are my best friend and one true love. There is still a part of me today that cannot believe that I'm the one who gets to marry you. Ashton, you are everything I have ever wanted and even more. I love you with all my heart," I said, trying hard not to cry but my voice still quivered.

"Layla, I promise to love and care for you, and I

will try in every way to be worthy of your love. I will always be honest with you, kind, patient, and forgiving. I promise to be a true and loyal friend to you. I will always try to make you happy, even if I have to make you mad at first. And most of all…I love you," Ashton said, smiling down at me. A few tears escaped my eyes and trailed down my face.

"Now, Ashton, repeat after me," the minister said. "I, Ashton, take thee, Layla, to be my wife, to have and to hold from this day forward, for better or for worse, for richer or for poorer, in sickness and in health, until death parts us. I promise to love and cherish you." Ashton repeated after him the whole time, smiling lovingly at me.

"Now, Layla, repeat after me." He turned to me now.

"I, Layla, take you, Ashton, to be my husband, to have and to hold from this day forward, for better or for worse, for richer or for poorer, in sickness and in health, until death parts us. I promise to love and to cherish you," I said.

"Can we now have the rings?" I turned to Kacey while Ashton turned to Nick. Placing the ring in my hand, she shot me a smile before I turned back around to face Ashton. He went first and placed a silver band on my ring finger. I grabbed his hand and slowly slid on the matching platinum silver ring on his finger. I'd gone to the ring store with Kacey, and she helped me pick out the perfect ring for Ashton.

"Now, Ashton, do you take Layla to be your wife?"

"I do," Ashton said.

"Layla, do you take Ashton to be your husband?"

"I do."

"I now pronounce you man and wife. You may kiss the bride." The minister finished. With a wide grin, Ashton leaned down and captured my lips with his. I kissed him back with so much passion that I almost forgot we had an audience until the sounds of yelling and whistling could be heard around us. We pulled apart, and I blushed while Ashton chuckled.

Hand in hand, we walked back down the aisle toward the house as all the guests clapped and shouted congratulations at us. We finally made it inside, and Ashton led me down and to his room. Once we reached it, he pushed me against the wall and leaned down to whisper in my ear.

"Hello, Mrs. Miller." His warm breath tickled my ear.

I shivered and breathlessly said, "We can't do that. We have guests waiting for us at the reception." Oh, how I wanted to forget about the reception, but I knew we couldn't; we had to see and greet the people who came.

"They can wait," he said, placing a kiss on my neck.

"They can, but your mother can't. She'll probably be here in a minute telling us to go." With a sigh, he rested his hand against my shoulder.

"Fine, but don't think that you're going to get any rest tonight," Ashton whispered huskily, pulling away and smirking at my flushed face. With a chuckle, he grabbed my hand and pulled me out of the room and outside toward where the reception was being held. On the way, I stopped and took off my heels, not wanting to walk in the sand in heels. My dress trailed behind me as we walked together.

The moment we got to the reception, we were surrounded by tons of people saying congrats and wishing us a happy marriage. After twenty minutes, we finally broke away, walking further in. I saw Kacey standing beside Nick, and with her was Neena and Liam, I immediately pulled Ashton toward them. Just as I was a few feet from them, Neena saw me and gave Kacey a look before they both practically ran toward me, engulfing me in a big hug. Once they let me go, Nick hugged me and so did Liam.

"You look amazing," they both said.

"Thank you." I grinned at them. They didn't look so bad themselves, dressed in black suits with matching flowers Neena and Kacey pinned to their suit jackets. Out of the corner of my eye, I saw Alex standing next to Ariel.

"Excuse me for a minute," I said to everyone, smiling at Ashton before making my way toward Alex. A few months after I broke things off with Alex, he ended up dating Ariel, Ashton's sister. Ashton wasn't at all fond of it, and after me talking to him for weeks about it, he accepted the idea and is slowly coming around to Alex, still not fully liking him. Seeing him and her together, I knew I did the right thing by him. They looked perfect with each other, and he seemed to really like her. Ariel knew about me and him, but since we didn't do anything but kiss once, she didn't mind. They now lived together, and I wouldn't be surprised if they get married soon.

"Hey," I said, getting their attention and hugging Alex.

"Hey. Layla, you look…" He trailed off, grinning down at me.

"Thank you. And thank you for coming too," I said.

"I wouldn't have missed it." He reached and wrapped his arm around Ariel's waist. Not wanting to bother them anymore or to leave Ashton's side any longer, I said I'd see them later and went back to Ashton, who in turn made sure to kiss me as soon as I got to his side. *Stupid, jealous man.*

"Can I have everyone's attention?" Clare said, standing up on a makeshift stage, holding a microphone, a band behind her. "Can we please clear the dance floor for the bride and groom's first dance." Slowly people began to move away, and Ashton led me to the dance floor. I was nervous about falling and embarrassing myself in front of all these people, but one look from Ashton, and I forgot about it all. "And to welcome the newlyweds, we have a surprise singer here to sing. Everyone, welcome Ed Sheeran." I gasped and looked at the stage as Ed Sheeran walked out, hugging Ashton's mom. I turned to Ashton with wide eyes.

"I wanted it to be a surprise," was all he said before wrapping his arm around my waist. My heart wanted to explode out of my chest as I grinned so hard up at him.

"Congratulations, Ashton and Layla Miller. This is for you," he said, and the band started playing. I instantly recognized the tune and leaned into Ashton wrapping my arms tight around me. "Thinking Out Loud" started playing as we swayed back and forth.

I closed my eyes, feeling safe and loved in the arms of the man I love. He is everything that I will ever need or would ever want. I would not go back and wish I didn't meet Ashton at that bar that night; if I had, I wouldn't have found the love of my life and be so happy. I wouldn't be dancing while Ed Sheeran sang to me on my wedding day, surrounded by my new family and new friends. It was okay parents weren't here because I was loved by an amazing man who I would never give up. I was right where I wanted to be.

Epilogue Part 2

Four months after the wedding

Layla

I paced back and forth in the bathroom, biting my fingernails waiting impatiently for the clock to hit its mark. I had been pacing the length of the bathroom for almost five minutes now, and my nerves had skyrocketed. *Why does the stupid box make you wait so damn long?* The whole time I had to wait, I thought back to Ashton and I's honeymoon and everything afterwards.

Ashton had surprised me with a trip to Barbados for our honeymoon the day after the wedding. He was so secretive about it that he didn't even let me pack my own bags; he got Kacey to do it. The moment we landed, I jumped in his arms remembering months before that we were talking about places we wanted to visit. I had said somewhere like Hawaii or Barbados, since I'd never been to a beach outside of New York.

To say the honeymoon was great was not even close; it was *incredible.* Ashton and I spent the first two days inside the hotel room, him not letting me out of the room, not even for food; that was delivered to us. Finally, on the third day, we left the hotel and walked around the shops down the street, trying to find stuff to bring back for Kacey, Neena, Liam, Ariel, and Alex. I promised I would find something, whether it be a snow globe or shirt. We lounged on the beach for hours and had some of the best food I had ever eaten. Ashton even got me to try seafood, which wasn't as bad as I thought.

We spent about a week and a half there before we had to leave. Work kept calling Ashton a few days before we left, and I could tell he was getting anxious to get back to work, wanting to make sure everything was going well. When we left I had a great tan, and was even more in love with Ashton than I ever thought possible.

He had changed so much from the guy I met over a year ago. He was more outgoing, affectionate, lively; basically, the total opposite of what he used to be. Of course, at work, he was still strict, but not too bad with me, thankfully. Even though sometimes he acted the way he used to, he soon came to realize it and apologized. Allie had broken him almost beyond compare, but over the last year I could see his blue eyes starting to shine again and he smiled more than he frowned.

Now as I paced the bathroom, I couldn't help but wonder what he was going to do. Was he going to be angry? Was he not going to still want me? I knew these thoughts were probably stupid, but I still couldn't help but think them. Yes, Ashton loved me and I him, but what would he think if this test showed positive? Were we even ready?

I was taking a pregnancy test. It had been too long since I'd had my last period, and I'd thrown up two days in a row. I tried to think of when we didn't use protection weeks ago, but I couldn't think of any. I mean, it's not like I didn't want children because I do, and I have even been thinking about it lately, but now that I was waiting for the results, I was nervous. Ashton and I just got married a few months ago, and he was busy with work, as was I. *Layla, just see what the test says before even thinking anything. For all you know, it could be negative.* The clock hit the ten minutes I had to wait, and I took a shaky breath before reaching for the stick. *Okay, this is it.* I looked down and took a deep breath.

"Babe, I'm home!" Ashton yelled from downstairs. I briefly heard him as he came toward the bedroom. I stared down at the pregnancy test, frozen. "Layla?" he called out again. "There you are." He came into the bathroom and walking toward me. "What are you doing?"

I looked up at him, my mouth wide open.

"Layla, are you okay?" he asked, concerned now. He still hadn't noticed the test in my hands.

"I-I, uh…" Swallowing, I forced out the words from my dry throat. "I'm pregnant." As soon as the words left my mouth, silence surrounded us and Ashton stared at me.

"What did you just say?" Now that my own shock was starting to die down a little, I was now concerned about Ashton's reaction. He stared at me in shock, his own expression matching mine.

"I'm pregnant." With him not saying anything, the thought that he didn't want children ran through my head. "Ash, please say something," I pleaded.

"Y-you're pregnant." Ashton said it like a statement than a question. He was staring blankly off to nowhere. *He doesn't want children,* I thought as a wave of sadness washed over me. The thought of Ashton not wanting a child with me cut me to the core. My hand moved to my flat stomach, almost like I could already feel the baby inside. I was just about to turn away, fighting back tears, when Ashton suddenly grinned widely and practically yelled.

"You're pregnant!" he yelled, coming at me and lifting my feet off the ground, twirling me around. Once he had set me back on my feet, I looked up at him.

"You're not mad or scared?" I asked.

"Why would I be? You're going to be having our child." He grinned at me. "I've always wanted children."

"You have?"

"Of course, and having one with you is all I could ever want." I smiled back at him, wrapping my arms around his waist and snuggling my head into his chest, his big arms wrapping around my own waist.

"We are going to have a baby," I whispered to myself.

After we stood there forever in the bathroom wrapped around one another, we finally pulled apart.

"We need to get you a doctor's appointment before we tell anyone." Ashton said exactly what I was thinking. I nodded along. I didn't want to tell anyone before we were a one hundred percent sure I was pregnant, and how far along I was. I knew the moment anyone heard about this they would go crazy, especially Kacey's and Ashton's moms. "I'll call the best OBGYN in the city and made an appointment as soon as possible."

"Okay, yeah." Ashton's hands worked their way down to my stomach. I smiled up at him, happy knowing he wasn't freaked out.

The next few days were hectic. Just two days after finding out I was pregnant, Ashton called the best OBGYN in the city and I got an appointment later in the afternoon. Even though I told Ashton he could stay at work and I'd just go, he wouldn't have it. While the doctor did the exam, it was very, very uncomfortable. She asked me a million questions. After the exam, she came back with the results and I was one hundred percent pregnant, almost two months to be exact; my due date was set for April twenty-seventh. She was fairly surprised that I hadn't experienced any morning sickness sooner than I had, or any other symptoms. I was just as surprised, but I couldn't be happier. We set up multiple appointments for the next few months to check up on my progress. Ashton wanted me to go almost every other week but with a firm no from me, he let up a little.

As we drove home that day, we decided we would tell everyone at the same time instead of separately. The rest of the week went by fairly quickly as I invited everyone over to our place this weekend, and I was busy at work. I wasn't at all that far along, but Ashton was already treating me like I was fragile. He even tried to get me to stop working. I appreciated the concern, but right now I was fine; I still had a long way to go. After arguing with him about working and treating me like I was fragile, he agreed to tone it down some, but he made me promise that when it got closer to my due date, I would stop working.

The weekend finally arrived, and all of Ashton's family was there, Nick included, as well as all of my friends: Kacey, Neena, Liam, and Alex. I had thought about telling them in a cool, fun way, but I wasn't the greatest at doing that, and it was too much work. Instead, Ashton and I decided to sit them all down and tell them straight forward. I was in the kitchen finishing putting some crackers, cheese, and different kinds of meat on a tray when Ashton scared me by wrapping his arms around my middle and resting his head on my shoulder.

"You ready?" he asked, pressing a soft kiss to my bare shoulder. I had bought a cute sundress a couple of months ago and decided that since I wouldn't be able to fit into it soon, I might as well wear it today, even if it wasn't that warm outside.

"I think so. Do you want to say or it me?" I asked, turning my head in his direction.

"I don't care. Whoever just wants to say it first when we get out there. It's going to be okay." He pulled away from me. Grabbing the tray, I stood on my tippy toes, giving him a small kiss before leaving the kitchen, Ashton on my heels. As I came to the living room, everyone was talking to one another, smiling. Setting the food on the coffee table, I took a step back relaxing a little as Ashton wrapped and arm around my waist and pulling me to him.

"Everyone," I said, first getting everyone's attention. Once everyone's eyes were on us, I froze, suddenly nervous. Biting my bottom lip, I looked up at Ash and he nodded down at me.

"We have some exciting news…Layla is pregnant," Ashton said. We stood there in silence as everyone took in what he just said. The first person to say anything was Kacey who jumped up yelling.

"I told ya so! You owe me twenty bucks!" she said, yelling down at Nick, Alex, and Liam. I stared at her confused, but the sound of a sob made me turn my gaze to Ashton's mother. She stood up and all but ran toward us, engulfing me in a huge hug.

"You're pregnant! I'm going to be a grandma!" She practically sobbed. I'd never seen Clare like this, usually she was the calm one.

"Congratulations, son," I heard Ashton's father say to him, but I couldn't see over Clare. "Honey, let go. She can't breathe." He pulled his wife off of me.

"Oh, honey, I am sorry. That can't be good for the baby!"

"No, no, Clare, it's okay," I said, smiling at her. Kacey pushed her way through everyone before flying at me almost making me fall.

"*You're pregnant!*" she yelled in my ear. She was hopping around while hugging the life out of me.

"Kacey, babe, she just said she is," Nick said, coming up to us. He and Ashton did their man hug thing, with Nick congratulating him. When Kacey wouldn't let me go, I looked over her shoulder to Nick for some help. He wrapped his arm around her waist and had to yank her off of me. "Babe, others want to hug her too," he said to a squirming Kacey in his arms.

"Congrats, Layla," Neena said, hugging me for a minute then stepping back.

"Thank you." I beamed at her.

"Seriously, Lay, congrats. You're going to make a great mom," Liam said, coming up behind Neena and giving me a side hug. They moved on toward Ashton as Ariel and Alex came toward me.

"Layla!" Ariel exclaimed, enveloping me in a hug like everyone else. "You and my brother are going to make a gorgeous baby." She pulled away from me so Alex could hug me.

"You guys really will," Alex agreed, smiling at me.

"Thank you, guys!" Once everyone had hugged Ashton and I and said congrats, I turned to Kacey not having forgotten about her earlier outburst.

"Kacey what did you mean 'You owe me twenty bucks'?" I asked.

"When you guys were on your honeymoon, I made a bet with the boys that you would be pregnant four months later, and *I won, baby!*" she yelled.

"You bet on us getting pregnant?" Ashton asked, looking at her and the boys.

"Hey, it's not my fault! It was her idea!" Liam said, holding his hands out.

"What did you guys bet then?" I asked him, Alex, and Nick.

"Well, I said once you get back you'll be pregnant," Nick said. "Liam said in two months, and Alex bet six months. Kacey said four, the closest so she won twenty bucks from all of us."

"You two didn't bet?" I turned to Neena and Ariel.

"Well…." Neena started looking guilty. "I kind of went with Liam's bet and Ariel went with Alex, so technically we did." I shook my head at my friends. Of course, they would bet on us.

"I said five months," John, Ashton's father, butted in suddenly. I turned to him, mouth wide. *Did everyone bet?*

"Dad!" Ashton exclaimed.

"Sorry, son, I overheard these kids talking and decided to add in too," he said with a shrug and a grin. Although Ashton's father was in his fifties, he still acted like a twenty-year-old. So out of everyone here, Ashton's mom was the only person who didn't bet on us.

The rest of the day went by fairly quickly as Clare talked about everything we will need for the baby, and how she planned on decorating a room for it too. After John calmed her down from her baby high, we spent the rest of the day talking and visiting.

The next few months flew by in a blur as I worked, went to doctor's appointments, and our new move. About a month or so into my pregnancy,

Ashton came home from work saying we should get a house instead of raising the baby in an apartment. The idea of having an actual house was nice, since I was starting to think the same thing about raising a child here. With both of us on board with the idea, we started looking around at houses a little bit away from the city, but not too far where Ashton or I would have to commute too far to work. Two weeks later, a real-estate agent was showing us a gorgeous two-story with a big back yard that had a pool. It had four rooms and three and a half baths, so Ashton could have a home office. The moment I stepped through the front door, I knew this was the house. Ashton loved it too, so we put a bid on it and a two days later we got it. It was in a nice neighborhood where the people seemed nice.

A few weeks after we told everyone, somehow the newspaper and magazines caught wind I was pregnant, splashing the news on the front page. Some made up stuff about how the baby wasn't Ashton's, but some foreign guy's. Of course, just like when me and Ashton got together, things slowly died down and more important news came up instead of the millionaire having a baby.

When I was eighteen weeks along, Ash and I went to our doctor's appointment knowing we could see if we were having a boy or a girl. We had discussed not finding out and waiting until he/she was born, but as we drove to the doctor's office, I decided, I wanted to know today. As the doctor took the ultrasound and we heard the heartbeat, I squeezed Ashton's hand. Even though I had heard the heartbeat plenty of times, every time I did my heart would speed up. As the time came to know the sex, Ashton and I looked at one another before nodding; we wanted to know. We were having a little boy! Ashton was over the moon after finding out we were going to have a boy, and in his own words, "I will have a son to throw a football with and go to fishing!" I was just as excited as Ashton and couldn't wait to see him.

Nearing the five-month mark, I really started to show and none of my clothes fit. Ashton found me one day crying in the middle of the closet, surrounded by clothes. I cried that none of them fit me and then when he said we can go shopping for new clothes, I got mad at him yelling that he thought I was fat. Yep, pregnancy hormones were in effect. Ashton, bless his heart, had been a good sport knowing what I was going through and not taking most of it to heart.

He had been great, especially when, at nine o'clock at night, I wanted chicken nuggets from McDonald's, and he went straight out and got some. Whenever I craved something, he was there to help. I tried being helpful when I could, and when my hormones started to die down I bawled on him, apologizing for my behavior.

One night while Ashton was still at work, I was sitting on the couch when a thought entered my mind. *What if I'm just like my parents? What if whatever made them hurt me seeped into me and I'd do that to my son?* I was a bawling mess when Ashton got home, and I could barely tell him what was wrong when he asked. When I told him my fears of becoming like my parents, he gripped my chin in a tight grip, forcing me to stare into his blue eyes.

"You are nothing like your parents. You are not going to hurt your son because that is not you. Your parents were messed up; you're not. Whatever happened to make them the way they were has nothing to do with you and it never will be. Layla, you are going to be a great mother," he told me fiercely. I kissed him hard after that and hung onto him for dear life. I knew he was right, but the thoughts sometimes still entered my mind.

I finally only had less than a month left, and Ashton forced me to stop working and stay home. I spent most of my days reading pregnancy books, hanging out with Kacey when I could as well as Ashton's mom, and eating. Everything was ready for when the baby came. His room was decorated, thanks to Clare, the walls a blue color, a crib in one corner, and a rocking chair in another. We had clothes from my baby shower in a dresser on one side, and toys in a basket on the other. By the front door we had a bag that had everything we would need whenever I went into labor, so we could just pick it up and be on our way to the hospital.

It was five and Ashton walked through the door as usual. I waddled over to him like a penguin, giving him a kiss on the lips.

"Something smells good," he said, taking off his suit jacket and setting it on the back of the couch.

"Thanks, I just finished dinner," I said, grinning and waddling back to the kitchen. I dished out the food on our plates and set them on the table. Ashton grabbed the silverware for me, and I reached up for the cups. Just as I extended my arm, I felt a flash of pain and wetness down my legs.

"Hey, honey, need some help with that?" Ashton asked from behind me. I turned with wide eyes to him.

"My water just broke." In a split second, Ashton was right in front of me, his eyes wide.

"Wait, what? Are you sure?" he asked, his voice panicky.

"No, I just like to get myself wet on purpose," I couldn't help but say sarcastically. He rolled his eyes but reached for my arm.

"We have to get you to the hospital!" He gently led me out of the kitchen, not even bothering with our food on the table, and grabbed the bag. "We are going to have our baby." He opened the door and turned to me.

"We are," I said, my eyes tearing up. He leaned down and kissed me before leading me outside and to the car. In just minutes, we were flying down the road to the hospital with him calling everyone. This was it. I was going to have my son.

Three years later

"Luke, be careful!" I yelled at my three-year-old son while putting down the plate full of hamburgers on the table outside.

"Luke, I'm coming for you!!" Liam yelled, bounding after my son toward the pool. I shook my head at him but smiled. We were having everyone over for a barbecue today for my twenty-seventh birthday and Ashton's twenty-ninth. Since we were born only a few weeks apart from one another, we decided to celebrate it together this year.

These past three years were the greatest years of my life so far. After giving birth to Luke on April nineteenth, everything in my life changed once again. I quit being Ashton's PA and started working on writing my own book, which was now out and has sold over a million copies. Ashton still runs his father's business, but lets a lot of the board members help so he could be home with me and Luke. About a year after having Luke, I found out I was pregnant again, this time with a girl, little miss Carter Miller. She was the light of my life.

"Mommy!" I heard Carter say my name. I turned and grinned as my husband walked toward me with my two-year-old daughter in his arms. Ashton didn't like to admit it, but Carter had him wrapped around her little finger. Anything she wanted he did, even if that meant dressing up in a princess dress and having tea. He denied that he ever did that, but with the photo, I took it was hard to deny. While Luke looked exactly like his dad, Carter took a little more after me. Luke was more loud and outgoing, while Carter was a little more shy and reserved. Both of my kids had brown hair, but Luke had my gray eyes while Carter had Ashton's bright blue ones. Both were going to be little heartbreakers just like their father was.

"Hey, baby." I pulled her out of Ashton's arms and into mine. "Did you help Daddy answer the door?"

"Ywes! Auntie Kay is here!" I kissed the top of her head before setting her down as she ran toward where Luke was wrestling Liam on the grass.

"Move, people! Fat pregnant woman coming through!" I heard Kacey before seeing her. I grinned as she wobbled over toward me. She was eight months pregnant with her second child, which they already named Elizabeth. Nick was right behind her, carrying their adorable two-year-old daughter, Macey, in his arms.

"Hey, Kay," I said, giving her a hug. "How are you?"

"Ready to pop," she replied but grinned at me. "Where's my favorite nephew?" she called out.

"On the lawn tackling Liam." I laughed. She made her way toward Luke as I hugged Nick.

"Macey!" I said, grabbing her as she reached out for me. She had light brown hair, a mix of Nick and Kacey's hair color, and green eyes she got from her father. After I had Luke, Nick and Kacey got married and, not soon after, were pregnant with Macey. Only two months after I had Carter, Macey was born. Just as Carter had Ashton around her finger, so did Macey. Nick loved his daughter and did practically whatever she wanted. At the age of twenty-seven, Kacey was working as the head designer at *Vogue* and Nick still ran his multimillion-dollar technology business.

I only held Macey a few minutes before Carter came running over, wanting to play with her. Since they were the same age they were the best of friends, just like Kacey and me. I looked over and saw Kacey sitting next to Neena, who was holding her one-year-old son, Mason.

Neena and Liam got married later than Kacey

and me. They got married two years ago and got pregnant with Mason a little while later. They were slower at starting a family besides me and Kacey. Their son Mason took after Liam so much it was almost uncanny. He had blonde hair and bright blue eyes, just like both parents. Neena didn't work at Miller Industries; instead, now she worked with Ashton's mother as a wedding designer, mostly designing wedding gowns. Liam now worked at Nick's company, helping him come up with new gadgets every month or so.

Our doorbell rang again, so I went inside and opened it, revealing Alex, Ariel, and Ashton's parents. After I gave Clare and John hugs, they went out back to say hi to everyone and their grandchildren. Wrapped in Ariel's arms was their new born son, Zach. These two dated for two years before Alex finally proposed and they got married. They just barely had their first child three months ago.

"Hey guys," I said, smiling down as Zach looked up at me. Even though he was only three months old, he looked just like Alex. "Everyone's out back," I said, gesturing behind me. As they walked outside with everyone else, I shut the front door and followed.

I stood in the doorway watching as Nick picked up Luke, throwing him into the pool. Carter was off in the grass with Macey, playing with their dolls and having a good time. Neena and Kacey stood around Ariel, looking at Zach and making faces at him. John sat at the table talking to Liam and Alex, while Clare played with Mason. And my husband stood beside the pool, grinning over at Luke and egging him on to get Nick in the water.

I smiled as I looked at everyone having a great time. When I was younger, I wanted a family just like this and now I had one. I had two amazing children and an equally amazing husband who stood by my side. I had two great in-laws, three best girlfriends, and three guy friends who had come to mean everything to me. This was everything I had ever wanted since I was little.

"What are you thinking about, babe?" Ashton's asked as he stepped in front of me, winding his arms around my waist as I wrapped mine around his neck.

"I'm thinking about how perfect my life is. This is everything I have ever wanted."

"Me too. You are everything I have ever wanted." He leaned down and kissed me. I kissed him back then turned us around, leaning against him.

I stared out to my backyard, smiling at everyone I love and knowing my life had turned out *exactly* how I wanted it, and I wouldn't change it for anything.

THE END

Acknowledgements

First, a huge thank you to everyone who read this book on Wattpad. This was the very first book I ever wrote four years ago. It is also the book that made me realize how much I enjoyed writing and wanted to become an author. Without the support and love from my readers on Wattpad, I wouldn't have published this book. So, this one is for you guys!

Also, thank you to my family once again for buying multiple copies and supporting me.

Lastly, thank you to my editors and everyone at Limitless for helping me with this whole process.

About the Author

Currently lives in a small town called Mesquite, Nevada. She is going to college to be an English teacher and writes on the side. When she isn't busy with school work or writing new books she likes to hang out with her family, do things outdoors, and read whatever she can get her hands on.

Facebook:
https://www.facebook.com/kenadee.bryant

Twitter:
https://twitter.com/kendoll350

Goodreads:
https://www.wattpad.com/user/OutOfMyLimit17